GETTING THE GOODS

GETTING THE GOODS

INFORMATION IN B.C. —
HOW TO FIND IT,
HOW TO USE IT

RICK OUSTON

NEW STAR BOOKS ■ VANCOUVER
1990

Printed and bound in Canada
1 2 3 4 5   94 93 92 91 90
First printing August 1990

The publisher is grateful for assistance provided by the Canada Council and the
Cultural Services Branch, Province of British Columbia

New Star Books Ltd.
2504 York Avenue
Vancouver, B.C.
V6K 1E3

Canadian Cataloguing in Publication Data

Ouston, Rick, 1955-
Getting the goods

ISBN 0-921586-06-x (bound). – ISBN 0-921586-05-1 (pbk.)
1. Information services – British Columbia – Handbooks, manuals, etc.
2. Information retrieval – Handbooks, manuals, etc.   3. Government information –
British Columbia – Handbooks, manuals, etc.   4. Research – Methodology –
Handbooks, manuals, etc.
I. Title.
Z674.5.C2088 1989   020'.9711   C89-091448-6

If they were a cribbage hand, they'd be a triple run worth fifteen points. Three Jacks – Wasserman and Webster, for showing how it's done – and Brooks, for spotting the holes. A Queen – Helen Morris, aka Slinger – for permitting it to be done. And a King: Gordon Sedawie, for convincing a high school dropout that even he could do it.

And for Nick Russell.

CONTENTS

Introduction..............1
Access to Information Act..............5
Adoptions..............9
Alternative Press..............13
Annual Reports..............16
Assessment Authority of B.C...............18
Background..............21
Bankruptcy..............23
Better Business Bureau..............25
B.C. Government..............28
Business Licenses..............34
Canadian Association of Journalists..............36
Canadian Radio-television and Telecommunications Commission..............38
Charities..............42
City Directories and Criss-Cross..............45
Competitors..............48
Computer Databases..............50
Contacts Influential..............54
Coroners..............57
Courts..............60

Cults..............65
Directory Assistance..............69
Dumpster Diving..............73
Environment..............77
Financial Disclosure Act..............81
Fire Commissioner..............84
Government Agent..............87
Investigative Reporters and Editors Inc...............89
Land Titles Office..............92
Landlords..............96
Minutes..............101
Off the Record..............104
Photocopy..............106
Professional Associations..............109
Public Accounts..............112
Registrar of Companies..............114
Regulatory Bodies..............117
Search Warrants..............119
Sources..............123
Ten-K..............125
Universities,..............130
Vancouver Stock Exchange..............135
Vancouver *Sun* and *Province*..............140
Who Owns What?..............144
Zen, And the Art of Putting It All Together..............149

INTRODUCTION

THE KID, A NEPHEW of a friend, had spent hours industriously scratching about in the rocks and dirt of the alley-way behind his house.

"What are you looking for?" my friend asked.

"Something to find," the kid said.

Something to find. Not the most scientific way of starting a search, but the kid had the right idea. If you're looking for information, you've got to do some digging. Instead of starting off blind, though, it usually helps to identify just what kind of rocks are available to turn over. That saves time and energy, and makes it more likely that you'll find something worth finding.

This book is designed to help you identify those rocks.

It began as a presentation to a seminar conducted by the B.C. branch of the Canadian Association of Journalists, for which I was asked to detail some of the sources that journalists use in tracking things down. The goal of the CAJ, as set out in 1978, is "to advance understanding of the concealed, obscure or complex aspects of matters that significantly affect the public." The key word in the motto is "concealed."

Usually, the hidden matters fall into two categories:

1 – Who did it and where are they? or

2 – Who owns it and where did the money go?

Easy questions. It's the answers that can be tough to find. But whether you're a journalist or a student, a lawyer or a private investigator, these are the kind of questions you face. Whether you're a reporter with five minutes to deadline, or an adoptee trying to track down family members, or a lawyer trying to find out just how your client's estranged spouse hid his or her ownership of that recreational property, these kind of questions play a role in your life.

Sometimes the task can appear daunting. Some of B.C.'s brighter minds are paid big dollars to hide things. But there are tools out there, tools available to anyone, which can make the task a lot easier. During the last dozen years working as a reporter for newspapers, magazines and television, I've found some of those tools, and ways to use them. They save time, money, and frustration. And once you get the hang of them, they're remarkably easy to use.

Most are public records, some supplied by government, some supplied by business interests. Some of the facts are collected for reasons far removed from any purposes that nosy investigators might have, but they can be turned toward those aims.

Understand this: anyone who owns anything, or spends anything, or who has any position in society, leaves a trail. As society becomes increasingly bureaucratized and computerized, that trail is recorded...somewhere. This book will help you find your way to that information.

Of course, if you use the methods and tricks outlined here, there's no guarantee of a successful hunt. I once spent a month scouring documents after getting a tip from an unimpeachable source that a powerful union leader was ripping off his membership. An impeccable investigation finally found...he had done no such thing.

In the following pages you'll find an alphabet soup of agencies, organizations and associations, all with information that's easily accessible and eminently helpful. Sometimes information is known and protected by individuals, so there are also some hints on how to pry that knowledge out of those people. Some of the information presented here may seem obvious and simplistic, but sometimes the way to the truth is obvious – so obvious that it's been sitting on the shelf waiting to be found, and no one's bothered to try to find it. For instance, CBC Radio reporter Barry Bell, a correspondent in Victoria, once ended the career of a cabinet minister when he reported a piece of public information which had been sitting – open to the public – in the legislative clerk's office for months. No one else had bothered to look at it (see FINANCIAL DISCLOSURE ACT).

Getting the Goods is geared to British Columbians finding things in their province, or to people wanting to find information about stuff going on in B.C. But because the world is an interconnected place, you'll also need some national and international sources. For a national view, I'd recommend the book Finding Canadian Facts Fast by Stephen Overbury. It's been recently updated, and is indispensable to anyone looking for things to find in this country.

This book has been divided into chapters outlining various sources of information, but for anyone sincerely interested in getting the goods, a request: read the whole thing. Successful researchers know that information is connected, and sometimes available where you'd least expect it. By the time you get to WHO OWNS WHAT, you should have absorbed enough tricks and sources to conduct your own investigations and find what you're looking for.

Finally, some words of caution to those reading this in a bookstore: by the time you buy this book, bits of it will already be out of date. Governments change, addresses change, policies change. Phone numbers included here were valid at the time of writing. They might be changed the minute you buy this book. I've made every attempt to provide up-to-date information, but we live in a changing society, and some of the addresses and practices will change too. If the phone number listed here is no longer in service, look up the new number and jot it down on the blank spaces on the pages of this book, or on the blank pages at the end of this volume.

Another caveat: this book won't tell you how to succeed in getting everything you want. Information about license plates used to be available for the asking, but now it's protected by the Ministry of Transportation which guards its files with a passion. The public cannot acquire information from ministry computers as private citizens. Some title search companies (see **LAND TITLES OFFICE**) are granted access to ministry files on license plates for commercial lawyers, but that entails enlisting the aid – and bill – of a lawyer. The police also have access to that information, and to information about criminal records of individuals, but the only way to pry the information out is to make friends with a police officer who will access the Canadian Police Information Computer as a personal favour. The public is not granted access to such information, so you'll have to use your powers of persuasion.

And if I haven't talked you out of buying this book, here's another warning: it's not complete. This is a guide to sources of information I've found during the years, compiled with help from other reporters who, working independently, have developed sources and tricks of their own. But I haven't found all the sources. Some of you reading this book will come across, or already know, other important sources of information. If you think the public should have access to that information too, share it by writing to me care of New Star Books. We can include it – with full credit given – in an updated version of *Getting The Goods*.

> Rick Ouston
> c/o New Star Books
> 2504 York Avenue
> Vancouver, B.C.
> V6K 1E3

What you do with any information, once you've found it, is up to you. But remember what Allan Fotheringham used to say: news isn't news unless someone doesn't want it told.

ACCESS TO
INFORMATION
ACT

THE OPPOSITION WAS BITTER, but the government was adamant: Canada would allow tests of the Cruise missile by the U.S. A 2,500-kilometre corridor across the true north strong and free would be used as a test path for the unarmed, nuclear-capable missiles. The ministers of External Affairs and of Defence both told a news conference that the tests were environmentally safe. Vancouver *Sun* reporter Glenn Bohn had a simple question: says who?

The ministers wouldn't say.

Bohn was not content to take the government's "no" for an answer. Reporters have become accustomed to the federal government's refusal to release information, but the Liberal government in 1983 passed a long-awaited law giving the public the right to request access to facts and data that the government had collected. The law was called the Access to Information Act, and it forced the government to make a certain amount of information available to Canadian citizens or landed immigrants. All you have to do is ask, and forward a $5 fee to the ministry which controls the information.

But it's not as easy as that. Bohn obtained an Access form from his local Canada Post office, included a cheque for $5, and wrote Ottawa, asking for the Cruise missile report. His request was rejected under one of the many clauses built into the Access Act which allows the government to keep things a secret. The Canadian government argued that the information had been obtained "in confidence from the U.S. Air Force," and that "the head of a government institution must refuse to disclose any record obtained in confidence from a foreign government unless that government consents to its release. Our consultation with U.S.A. authorities revealed they would not consent to our releasing the record requested, consequently access must be denied."

The Access Act contains provisions for appeals, and Bohn appealed. And appealed. And appealed. And each time, he was turned down. The Defence Department stonewalled.

Finally, a year after the initial request, Bohn got a phone call from a contact who had been poking around the Vancouver Public Library. There, on the shelf, was the environmental evaluation study of the Cruise missile tests.

It seems that, while the official view of the Defence Department was to keep the report a secret, copies had been sent to main library branches across the country. After a year-long struggle with the bureaucracy of the federal government to tell the public why Cruise missile testing was safe, Bohn got what he wanted...with his library card.

That's not to say that the Access to Information Act is useless. Reporters and environmentalists have used the act to unearth masses of previously hidden details from Ottawa, on topics ranging from Brian Mulroney's travel budget to internal studies of prison riots. But since the act was passed in 1983, the government has tightened restrictions, making it harder and harder to use the Access Act to uncover information that might embarrass someone.

How does the act work? In simplest terms, the researcher identifies the records that are needed, and the government agency which controls them. The researcher writes to that department and requests that the information be released. There is a fee of $5 for each request, and photocopying fees for the information provided, unless the department agrees to waive those fees because the information is in the public interest. Legally, the information should be produced within 30 days. But, as was the case with Bohn's hunt for the elusive environmental impact report, the government has the right to extend that time limit – a right it usually takes advantage of.

Researchers who feel the government is unfairly delaying coming up with the goods – or is just straight refusing to comply – can appeal to the office of the Information Commissioner in Ottawa. On paper, the process sounds simple, but it can be a complex and costly exercise. Toronto lawyer Heather Mitchell and University of Victoria professor Murray Rankin have produced a valuable guide called *Using the Access to Information Act* (published by International Self-Counsel Press) which explains in detail the various procedures and pitfalls of the act. Mitchell and Rankin conclude there are too many restrictions in the act, that "they overlap each other, and they are confusing and difficult to understand." Nevertheless, the act can be a worthwhile tool, particularly if the researcher follows the steps in their book.

However, a word of caution is needed: I would suggest using the Access Act only as a final resort. If the federal government has information you need, that information is often available through other sources, maybe from a friendly MP, maybe a provincial ministry, maybe a university – or even your local library.

Once you initiate an official Access Act request, the government starts thinking of ways and methods of keeping its zealously guarded information a secret, and can seal, stall and stonewall forever. Bureaucrats button up when an access request is made, and people who might have been willing to release information on an informal basis find their hands tied.

I once waited for months while the government refused to release a report on convicted Nazi war criminal Jacob Luitjens. Finally, in desperation, I phoned a local MP to see what he could find. Within 24 hours, I had the report in my hands. It had been released to members of Parliament months earlier, before the government got cold feet. The MP had the report in his files, and gave it to me. Six months later, the federal Department of External Affairs grudgingly released the same report in compliance with the Access Act.

And note: there is no provincial equivalent to the Access to Information Act. Various B.C. statutes force the provincial government to reveal some information about its activities, but there is no overriding rule about releasing information about provincial affairs. Some municipal governments, like Vancouver's, have Freedom of Information laws giving the public access to whatever information it collects – with the exception of personnel matters – but B.C. has not agreed with the concept of the public's right to know.

ADOPTIONS

THE ANCIENT SUMERIANS thought that adoptions should be kept secret. The penalty for people disclosing information about adoptions was harsh: their tongues were cut out. That kind of eye-for-an-eye, tongue-for-a-fact justice is outmoded now, but the secrecy behind adoptions continues.

Canadian governments, B.C.'s included, jealously guard the information they hold about adoptees. The files are locked away, hidden from people who want to know the facts of their lives. Even the simplest information is kept a secret, down to the original names of adoptees. Unless adoptees are fortunate enough to learn of their original names from the adoption papers signed by their adoptive parents, they will likely never know even the barest of details.

The information is also hidden from the mothers and fathers who gave their children up for adoption. While it might have been a decision borne of poverty or shame or desperation, those parents who renounced their rights are never given the opportunity to reconsider their actions.

It wasn't always like that. Before the 1960s, most adoptions were handled by private agencies. Each agency managed its records differently. Some were willing to divulge information to adult adoptees or their parents, some weren't. The rules were standardized when the B.C. government took over the business of adoption in the 1960s. Adoption files were forwarded to the government, never to be seen again. In 1988, B.C. started what most other provinces already had – an adoption reunification registry. It's a grand title, but the program has one huge and basic flaw. In the terminology favoured by bureaucrats, the registry is "passive." That means that both sides, the adult adoptee plus his or her biological parent, must register with the program. If that happens, both sides will be contacted and a reunion made possible. The passivity of the registry means that it won't work if one side doesn't bother, for whatever reasons, to register.

To join the registry, applicants must pick up a form at their local Vital Statistics office. (See the blue pages of your telephone book for the office nearest you.) Vital Statistics also offers a toll-free number – 1-800-663-8328. You will be mailed an application form if you phone that number and ask for one. The B.C. government charges a $25 fee for joining the registry, and there is no guarantee of a successful reunion. Still, it's a start.

Whether the government has the moral right to keep such information a secret is a question open to debate. Radio broadcaster Barrie Clark, who has written a book on his successful search for a daughter who had been given up for adoption, argues that concerned people should pressure the government to change its rules. He is supported by groups such as the Canadian Adoptees Reform Association and Parent Finders, but, so far, the government hasn't changed its policies.

The B.C. Ministry of Social Services, however, will make some information available to inquiring adult adoptees. Regional offices of the ministry – see the blue pages under Social Services – will reveal information which social workers deem "non-identifying." That usually includes the ages and social backgrounds of parents, where they were born, number of brothers and sisters, and medical information that the workers feel is pertinent.

But no names.

However, those scanty details sometimes are enough to help a committed adoptee play detective. I know. I was adopted, and I found my mother through that "non-identifying information" and the assistance of my adoptive parents.

While each search will be as different as the lives of the people involved, what follows is how I did it, through the use of public sources that were freely available . . . and almost free of charge. People searching for their own parents or children would have to adapt the techniques and procedures to their own circumstances and histories, but the basic idea is the same: the information is there. All you have to do is use it. It's easy, once you get the hang of it, and it's effective.

My adoptive parents gave me access to my adoption papers, which contained my original surname. They figured, as I do, that it was my right to have the fact of my name. (Because we're dealing with a true story – my own – involving real people, I've got to keep the name a secret. Let's say it was Brown.)

The "non-identifying information" provided by the B.C. government included three pieces of solid information: my mother's birthday, the fact that her father died two years before I was born, and the province in which she was born. Not much to go on, but, as it turned out, more than enough.

Each province maintains a Department of Vital Statistics which records marriages, births, and deaths. Information is usually made available only to family members, but since the subject is adoption, it's all in the family anyway. I wrote to the Vital Statistics office in the province where my mother was born, asking for a record of the birth of a female infant named Brown for the year my mother was born. I also asked for the record of the death of a man named Brown who died two years before I was born (remember, that was mentioned in the "non-identifying information").

Within two weeks I received a response: the Vital Statistics office had records for a woman named Brown for that year, and a death certificate of a man named Brown for the proper year. Birth records usually contain the city or town in which the person was born, and this one did. The death certificate gave me the precise day, month and year of the death.

I then contacted the library in that city, asking a librarian to look at the microfiched back issues of the newspaper for a news story or obituary notice – usually found in the classified advertising section – for a man named Brown who died on that date. The librarian found the obituary later that day. The obituary contained the names of Mr. Brown's children. One of the names corresponded with the name on the birth certificate. The telephone directory for that city did not have a listing for the woman, but it did have a listing for one of the other names given in the obituary. I telephoned that person and asked where I could find his sister.

He told me. I telephoned my mother, and we cried.

Adoptees looking for their parents will find potential sources of information scattered throughout this book.

The B.C. Department of Vital Statistics can be written to at:

Vital Statistics Division
1515 Blanshard Street
Parliament Buildings
Victoria, B.C.
V8V 1X4

Parent Finders operates its own national reunion registry. It can be contacted at:

Parent Finders
3960 Westridge Avenue
West Vancouver, B.C.
V7V 3H7
(604) 437-1028 (Vancouver)
or (604) 642-6122 (Sooke)

Canadian Adoptees Reform Association operates its own, smaller registry:

Contact CARA at (604) 277-8255

ALTERNATIVE PRESS

IT LOOKED LIKE a pretty good story at the time. No one knew just how big it would grow. In spring 1983, *Newsweek* was carrying a report on a strange new disease which seemed to afflict homosexuals, Haitians, and intravenous drug users in the U.S. An editor pointed out the *Newsweek* story and asked me to find out if there were any cases in B.C. After phoning hospitals, gay organizations, coroners, and doctors, it became obvious that there were. Two people in B.C. had already died of the disease which doctors had labeled with the acronym AIDS, for Acquired Immune Deficiency Syndrome. My report in the Vancouver *Sun* was a Canadian first, a journalistic coup of which I was proud.

Proud, that is, until the next week, when I started a follow story. I came across a Vancouver monthly newspaper *Angles*, serving the gay community. *Angles*, it turned out, had been reporting on the AIDS story for a year, carrying reports from around the world, distributed through the gay grapevine. Readers of *Angles* already knew what had been trumpeted on the front page of the *Sun*: there was a new disease, it was deadly, it might be connected to sex.

Before the *Newsweek* story and my subsequent investigation, I had never heard of *Angles*, and it turned out I wasn't alone. Although thousands of people had been reading *Angles* voraciously, us supposedly informed and connected news professionals working in Vancouver hadn't been paying attention to a source of news available in our own backyard. *Angles* had covered the AIDS issue because it was of interest to its readers. But the high-paid journalists in Vancouver, myself among them, were confining themselves to the established, mainstream news sources – the *Sun*, the *Province*, the *Globe and Mail*, Canadian Press, Associated Press, newsmagazines and TV news shows – without trying to become informed about what else was going on out there.

The AIDS story didn't surface in the mainstream news media until 1983. If we had been on top of our job, reading material from different sources, looking for things to find, the story would have surfaced earlier. That means people would have been informed earlier. That means they might have taken precautions earlier, preventative measures which might have limited the spread of the disease. People who ran the risk of acquiring the disease would have been urged earlier to stop donating blood.

And that means lives would have been saved.

Not all news stories are a matter of life and death, but the mainstream media often lags behind the alternative press. And that means that long before something becomes an issue in the mainstream media, it's probable that smaller publications out there have already carried at least some information in their pages.

Whether it's *Angles* for gay news, *Kinesis* for women's issues, *New Directions* for well-informed – albeit slanted toward the NDP – commentary and analysis (and try Toronto-based *This Magazine* for national stories which often touch on B.C. issues), or the various publications of the conservative Fraser Institute, there's a good chance that the so-called "alternative press" has already beaten the socks off the established press, and that the information is just sitting there, waiting to be read.

In B.C., such publications as *Equity* Magazine (business) and the *Georgia Straight* (entertainment) might have already carried information on the thing you're looking for. Most public libraries carry back issues of B.C.'s alternative press. Take a look.

Overbury's *Finding Canadian Facts Fast* contains a helpful chapter on using indexes – such as the *Canadian Periodical Index* and the *Canadian Business Index* – to save the time it takes skimming through back issues of old magazines. The indexes tell you where stories can be found on the topic you're looking for. To determine if a particular magazine is indexed or not, take a look at Ulrich's *International Periodicals Directory* or *The Standard Periodical Directory*. Yes. . . those are both indexes of indexes.

ANNUAL REPORTS

EVERY SOCIETY AND COMPANY issues an annual report, either because they're trying to woo prospective investors and customers, or because the provincial government says they have to under obligations of the B.C. Societies Act.

Annual reports are a good place to start research on a company which might be polluting your river or making questionable payments to local aldermen. The reports will give you names of company or society officials, projects the company is working on, and other corporate interests in which the company might be involved.

Usually, the reports will paint the rosiest picture possible of the organization... how sales are up, how membership is up, how the future couldn't be better. Often they are little more than corporate propaganda at its worst, and that's why they're readily available from the society's offices and often the public library. But sometimes these innocuous pieces of fiction will help you find your way to the truth.

In 1983 I was assigned to find out what was going wrong with the Vancouver Symphony Orchestra. It was making more money than ever before, but its deficit was rising like never before, and one of B.C.'s premier artistic endeavours was in danger of tooting its horn no more. None of the official spokespeople would say why. But the annual report, like most annual reports, also contained a list of names – in the VSO's case, a list of symphony staff and orchestra members, dozens of names of insiders. It then became a matter of looking up those names in the telephone book and dialing the phone. I asked for help and for background, and people said no and said no and said no, until someone – we dubbed him Deep Note – said yes.

It was Deep Note who pointed out discrepancies in the financial statements, who passed on information about secret loans to high-ranking VSO officials, and who finally helped uncover enough information to cause the symphony society to re-examine its actions and clean up its act. Deep Note operated not out of malice, but out of concern for the future of his symphony. Like many people, he had heard gossip and stories, and he passed them on to where they'd do some good.

The moral of Deep Note is that you don't need to start off with "sources" – sources are usually just a phone call away. It's just a matter of looking, and annual reports will give you the names of people to look at.

A hint: if you've exhausted the list of names in the annual report without finding any talkative sources, take a look at out-of-date annual reports which contain names of former employees and officials. Often it's people who have left the company who will be most willing to chat. This method also works for government telephone books – a good way to find a former deputy minister who might now be willing to disclose.

ASSESSMENT
AUTHORITY
OF B.C.

LAND IS OFTEN THE MOST controversial part of B.C. politics, whether it's a municipality rezoning property for a hospital or the provincial government selling the Expo site to Hong Kong investor Li Ka-Shing. Land is where the dollars are . . . and often where the scandals are.

The trick comes in finding those scandals. The best place to start is the Assessment Authority of B.C., says Donald Gutstein, a journalist and academic. Gutstein is probably B.C.'s best digger of information about land. It was Gutstein who pieced together Vancouver Mayor Gordon Campbell's work for Marathon Realty in the days before Campbell became mayor of the city now dealing with Marathon's development applications. And it's Gutstein who tells *Vancouver* Magazine readers about who owns the most expensive homes in the city – much to the dismay of the owners, who try to keep such things a secret. Gutstein believes the ownership and development of land is the core of municipal news coverage, and he agrees with writer James Lorimer, whose 1972 book *A Citizen's Guide to City Politics* argues that the essence of local government is real estate.

Gutstein says that city hall mainly does two things:

(1) provides services to property such as water, sewers, garbage collection, police and fire protection;

(2) regulates the use of land through planning, zoning, building bylaws, minimum standards.

In return, the major source of city revenues (about 50 to 60 percent) is the property tax. Because city hall is so important to developers and owners of land, they want to control it – or at least influence council's decisions.

"In virtually every municipality in B.C. you'll find real estate types on the local councils." The most notorious in B.C. was former Surrey mayor Ed McKitka, who went to jail for feeding his municipality's secret sewer plans to his developer employer. But B.C. has a few developers in other prominent positions as well. "The premier [Bill Vander Zalm], mayor of Surrey before McKitka, is primarily a developer," Gutstein says. "Fantasy Gardens is really a story about increased wealth as a result of getting land removed from the Agricultural Land Reserve and getting it rezoned by Richmond council." Former premier Bill Bennett is better known for his stock market dabbling, but he's also a land developer. And former Health minister Peter Dueck is a Fraser Valley land developer. Says Gutstein: "Hospitals are certainly about health, but hospitals are also occupiers of key pieces of land, often with ambitious expansion plans."

So, if the local municipal council is thinking of rezoning Main Street, or hospital hill, to allow for commercial development, you might want to visit your local Assessment Authority office to find out just who will benefit.

(Note: city halls also keep a copy of the assessment rolls. You have to visit the offices in person – clerks at the Assessment Authority won't look things up for you by phone.)

The Assessment Authority tells you:
– The owner of the property
– The assessed value
– The size of the property
– Its legal description

Every two years, the Assessment Authority assesses each piece of property under its jurisdiction and mails out assessment notices to property tax payers. The assessed value of the property is supposed to be its market value – what the property would sell for at the time the assessment was done. That value is what property taxes are based on. But a word of caution is needed here: in a rising market, assessments are generally much lower than sale prices, so you can't say the land is "worth" its assessed value – only that it was assessed at such a value.

All assessment records are public, says Gutstein, "and more important, no fee is charged to inspect records. That's why I use this source as much as possible."

The assessment office also keeps a computerized alphabetical list of owners in the municipality, so if you're looking to find if someone owns property in your area, that's the place to start. The list is also handy for determining if a company owns land in the area. Recalcitrant husbands have been known to hide their ownership of recreational property behind a company name so it doesn't turn up listed under their name. But if you know the names of the man's companies, you can use the computer to find out if the company holds land in the area served by the local office of the Assessment Authority. Then (see REGISTRAR OF COMPANIES) confirm the ownership of the company.

There are offices of the B.C. Assessment Authority in every community in B.C. For locations of the offices serving the area you're looking at, consult the white pages of your phone book under the heading B.C. Assessment Authority.

A little known fact for researchers trying to dig up information about land in Vancouver on Sunday: the main branch of the Vancouver Public Library carries a microfiche copy of old assessment rolls. The information might be one or two years out of date, but the library is open on Sunday, while the Assessment Authority of B.C. operates just on weekdays. If you're battling a deadline and looking for information on a Vancouver address – say a Vancouver Eastside hotel has burned down during the weekend and you're hunting for the owner of the firetrap – a visit to the library might uncover what you need. Some libraries in other communities throughout B.C. carry old tax assessments for their community. (Also see COMPUTER DATABASES.)

BACKGROUND

THE TERM 'BACKGROUND' is important to journalists, and to anyone who might wind up talking to journalists. It won't help you find information, but it will help you use it without getting into trouble. Usually when people communicate with each other, the information is for the record. All of it can be used, and the source can be revealed. It is an accepted standard of practice that all communication is for the record – unless the source and interviewer reach an agreement *before* both sides start talking. (See **OFF THE RECORD** for an important distinction.)

Sometimes information is sensitive, and the source does not want to be revealed publicly. Maybe the sources are leaking information about their jobs that could get them fired if the bosses found out. Maybe the source is revealing information about a neighbour that could start a feud if a name is used. In that case, both sides can agree to talk on background. That understanding means that anything the source says can be used, but the identity of the source cannot be made public. Most newsrooms require that a reporter who wishes to attribute a fact to an unidentified source must reveal the name of the source to at least one other person in the news operation – usually the senior editor.

Right now in Canada, journalists have no legal right to refuse to identify a source if ordered to do so by a judge. One day, the

Supreme Court of Canada may decide to rule that the "freedom of the press" clause in the Charter of Rights and Freedoms does give the news media the right to keep sources a secret, but for now, any reporter who refuses a judge's order to reveal a source could wind up in jail, guilty of contempt of court.

It has been a matter of luck that very few judges have decided to push the issue. And that means that a reporter who agrees to talk for background is also agreeing to go to jail if necessary to protect the source.

BANKRUPTCY

A SHARP-EYED VANCOUVER *Sun* printer noticed the tiny ad in the newspaper's classified "legal" section: a man named Laurier LaPierre was filing for bankruptcy. The outspoken journalist was still hosting CKVU-TV's *Vancouver Show*, offering his opinion on a wide range of topics, but it looked like LaPierre's personal life, at least economically, was not as successful as it could be. Repeated telephone calls, and even a personal visit to his television station elicited a "no comment" from the man who was once a national star for his work on *This Hour Has Seven Days*.

Bankruptcies in Canada are a national affair, handled through a department of the federal Consumer and Corporate Affairs ministry called the Superintendent of Bankruptcy. Unlike most federal government agencies, the Bankruptcy office keeps open files – available to anyone who chooses to look.

A look inside LaPierre's file revealed the darkest secrets of the broadcaster's personal finances. He owed back taxes to Revenue Canada, and payments to credit cards. He owed money to his accountant, to law firms, and to department stores. He even owed his drycleaner. It was a story that was sad, if not sensational, and it could be told because the information was available to the public.

Chances are that you will rarely have reason to explore the personal finances of a television celebrity, but keep this in mind:

before lending money to, or investing money with, anyone, it is worthwhile to check if your prospective business partner has ever filed for bankruptcy. It's fast, it's easy, it's legal. . .and it's free. In fact, for reasons known only to the federal government, it's probably the simplest personal information which can be acquired on anyone. You can visit the District Insolvency Office in downtown Vancouver in person, or ask for a search by mail. The helpful folks at Consumer and Corporate Affairs will even do a search for you over the phone.

Copies of the relevant information are kept on microfiche and computer records. The original documents are eventually sent to the B.C. Supreme Court for filing (see COURTS).

So, remember: never a borrower or a lender be. . .at least, not without checking the person's financial history first. The fact that someone hasn't filed for bankruptcy is no guarantee of that person's financial success, but it's a good thing to examine.

Bankruptcy Office
Suite 1440
800 Burrard Street
Vancouver, B.C.
V6Z 2H8
(604) 666-5007

BETTER
BUSINESS
BUREAU

JOE HARGITT IS a Vancouver businessman who sells companies. Nothing unique there, except for the nature of the companies that Joe Hargitt sells. They have no assets. No holdings. Nothing at all. In fact, they are little more than legal pieces of paper saying that a company name has been incorporated and registered. The businesses have no monetary value. Nevertheless, investors continue buying companies from Joe Hargitt. What they get in return for their money is a piece of paper, signed by Hargitt, promising to turn over 51 percent of the "company" to the investor.

Sometimes Hargitt tells potential investors that the company is in the business of selling advertising on shirtboards – those cardboard inserts that drycleaners insert into a freshly laundered shirt. Sometimes Hargitt tells investors they are buying a company which sells advertising to promote a radio station, or advertising packages for people to read on the Amtrak train from Seattle to Vancouver. Hargitt usually doesn't tell investors that Amtrak doesn't travel between Vancouver and Seattle.

And usually his investors don't bother to ask.

That is, they don't ask questions before it's too late, and before they realize they have given money to Joe Hargitt and have only a piece of paper to show for it. By then, they can kiss their money goodbye. Hargitt has, under the law, fulfilled his part of the bargain – he has turned over 51 percent of the "company," and investors are left holding the paper, licking their wounds, and feeling pretty stupid.

The investors thought they were buying something of value, a company which would immediately start paying dividends. The story they got from Joe Hargitt sounded good, plausible, profitable. But they listened only to Joe and did not bother to check out the story with anyone else. Within a few weeks, they usually realize that there are no dividends to come. By then it's too late.

Many have launched civil actions, but the standard reaction of lawyers is to advise the hapless investors that it would cost them more to push the matter through the courts than they've already lost. A legal action would throw good money after bad.

I visited Joe Hargitt one day to ask him about the way he made his money, and about the hundreds of thousands of dollars he had made selling his "companies." Hargitt laughed and recited an old maxim: "First you hustle, then you get honest, then you get honoured," he said. "We're almost honest."

The next time I visited Joe, he hit me. On camera.

Caveat emptor. Buyer beware. Latin might be a dead language, but the ancients wouldn't have come up with a phrase like that unless the Caesars had their own version of Joe Hargitt. What the Caesars didn't have was Kaye Baker, head of the Better Business Bureau of B.C. In an age where information is increasingly shoved onto floppy disks and forgotten (see COMPUTER DATA-BASES), Kaye Baker retains the old ways. Her filing cabinets are stuffed with old files, yellowed newspaper clippings and complaints which detail the activities of the men and women in B.C. for whom the buying public should beware.

Baker can walk to a filing cabinet, open a drawer, and produce a dossier on hundreds of people. Under the Hs, Baker's files show that Hargitt was selling his shirtboard "company" back in 1959, the same year he was convicted of fraud involving used cars. He was convicted again in 1964, again for fraud, again for used cars. Between 1959 and today he's sold the shirtboard company at least a dozen times. He's also been convicted of practising law without a license.

This is not a man with the kind of credentials that most people would choose to give money to. But Hargitt keeps his background to himself. Kaye Baker knows Joe Hargitt's background, and can advise potential investors about the background of a salesman or company like Hargitt. Her advice, and her knowledge, is free to the public. All people have to do is call. To Baker's chagrin, too often they don't.

Baker occasionally opens her files to researchers, and has helped several reporters dig up information about questionable companies – information which has saved potential buyers from possible losses. One of her specialties is getting to the truth of advertising campaigns which seem to offer a good or service at a price too good to be true.

"If it sounds too good to be true," says Baker, "it usually is."

Sadly, the Better Business Bureau has been in perilous financial shape for years. The BBB relies on membership fees from corporations for its income. As the consumer rights movement of the late sixties has waned, more and more companies have decided that they don't need the hassle of joining the BBB, which demands that companies resolve consumer complaints to the satisfaction of the bureau. The B.C. Department of Consumer Affairs has been gutted the past few years, rendered almost ineffective, so the BBB has become the last resort of consumer protection.

For now, Kaye Baker is still in business. Joe Hargitt is, too.

The Better Business Bureau, Kaye Baker
404-788 Beatty Street
Vancouver, B.C.
V6B 2M1
(604) 681-0312

For general information about consumer goods and services, you might also try the files of the B.C. branch of the Consumers' Association of Canada, a non-profit society aimed at protecting consumer's rights. Volunteer members of the organization can be contacted in Vancouver at (604) 682-3535 or (604) 682-2920.

B.C. GOVERNMENT

NO ONE GENERATES PAPER better than a bureaucrat. Corporate bureaucrats are bad. Civil service bureaucrats are worse. It is their job to generate paper. Memos. Reports. Supplements. Glossaries. Inquiries. Annual reports. Updates. Summaries. Studies. Examinations. Directories. Manuals. Statutes. Somewhere in that mass of paper is, oftentimes, the nugget of information you're looking for. The problem is finding it.

The provincial government regulates many of our human endeavours. From health care to highways, education to forests, mining to liquor stores – a B.C. bureaucrat is in charge of them all. Those bureaucrats, and the cabinet ministers who are their political masters, control and monitor our schools and roads, our mines and trees, our hospitals and our provincial tax dollars. That process includes keeping track of spending, trends, policy, societal impact, and laws. It is a big job, running a province. It is a job that creates a huge paper trail. That trail can be followed, but it can be frustrating as hell.

Unlike the federal government (see ACCESS TO INFORMATION ACT), B.C. has no freedom of information law. That means the citizens of this province have no legal right to acquire any of the information the government collects. Various ministries and their subsidiaries have policies mandating the release of certain information, but policies are changeable, often at the whim of the bureaucrat, minister, or premier of the day. Sometimes provincial government departments are surprisingly open and free. Sometimes they can be exasperatingly secretive.

There are some people, like University of Victoria law professor Murray Rankin, who argue that B.C. should follow the lead of other provinces and create its own access to information law. Others argue that such a law could be used to keep even more information secret, as has been the case with the federal Access Act, and the Freedom Of Information law in the U.S. For now, the argument is academic because there is no law. We're left to our own devices.

You can be sure that if a piece of information seems important and worth having, it is available someplace, somewhere, inside the B.C. government. It's your job to figure out where.

The first stop, and most important tool, is the Government of British Columbia Phone Directory. It is available in most public libraries, and copies can be purchased from most major book stores for $6. Buy one. This 205-page phone book lists the name and department of every notable civil servant in the province. Just as important, the government phone book provides a graphic glimpse into the internal workings of ministries. The phone book separates the various departments inside the ministry, giving the eager researcher a chance to find out just who is in charge of what.

For example, people seeking information about the Liquor Control and Licensing Branch may be surprised to learn that the once-powerful liquor branch now falls under the Ministry of Labour and Consumer Services. What does liquor have to do with labour? Not much. Except that liquor was once controlled by the now-defunct Ministry of Consumer and Corporate Affairs. That ministry was scrapped when Premier Bill Vander Zalm tried to "streamline" his government, and portions of the ministry were parceled out to other departments. Labour Minister Lyall Hanson wound up in charge of the province's liquor stores and pub licenses when he was still trying to learn how the B.C. Labour Code worked.

Maybe that explains how Hanson cleared his department of any wrongdoing during the Knight Street Pub fiasco, when the premier's right-hand man, David Poole, leaned on a civil servant to get a pub license for a friend. Hanson investigated and found nothing amiss. Reporters at BCTV pushed the story, knocking on doors around the neighbourhood and learning that several ballots in the referendum on the pub had been forged. The station's investigation prompted the B.C. Ombudsman's office to investigate. Ombudsman Stephen Owen discovered enough shady dealings to prompt the resignation of the liquor branch general manager. Poole also quit. People who worked on the referendum were convicted.

If the minister in charge has a hard time figuring out how his ministry runs, that means the lowly researcher might also find it difficult. Difficult, but not impossible. On the face of it, it's remarkably simple. If you're a journalist or researcher, you must first contact the public relations office of the ministry involved. Each ministry maintains such an office. Names and phone numbers change with the seasons, with governments, with cabinet shuffles, so there's no point to list them here; the numbers would soon be out of date. Refer to your government phone book. The departments are sometimes called the Information Services division, sometimes Public Affairs, sometimes Public Relations. The so-called "information officers" in those departments do the job they're told to do by the minister or deputy minister in charge.

Some information officers take their job description seriously. They truly believe it is their job to provide information to the public, and they will be as helpful as possible, even to the point of suggesting ways and methods the researcher hasn't thought of.

Others are true to the nickname of the public relations officer: flak. That's short for flak-catcher – the heavy flak jackets that soldiers wear to reduce injury when they're hit by shrapnel. These "information officers" believe it is their duty to protect the backsides of their political masters by withholding information. They are not helpful. Approach them with care. Sometimes they will hinder, obfuscate, and downright fib to do the job they feel they must do. Sometimes information officers will just be plain lazy and will tell you they don't know the answer. Don't accept that. It is the information officer's job to find the answer. Or at least to direct you to someone who might know. Be polite, but firm. And it's been said before, but remember: Don't take "no" for an answer. If they say "no," ask them, "How come?" Unhelpful people, even government bureaucrats, can often be jogged into assistance if asked to justify themselves.

The biggest trick in a flak's big bag of tricks is the no-answer answer. That's where the flak will try to ward off a question by responding with an answer that has little, if anything, to do with the original question. Don't let them get away with that. The best way to approach an unknown information officer is to develop your question, or questions, before calling the information office. The better prepared you are, the less likely the officer will be able to duck the answer. You must have a pretty good idea of what you want to get, and don't hang up until you've got some cooperation.

In some ministries, the information officer will already know the answer to what you're looking for. In others, the officer will have to check with the bureaucrat involved. Life would be much easier if researchers could contact the bureaucrat in question directly, but usually that's not possible. Most ministries have developed a policy requiring reporters and researchers to clear their question through the information officer as a first step before any action is taken. After that's done, one of several things can happen: the flak can tell you the answer; the flak can check for the answer; the flak can direct you to the bureaucrat involved and permit you to talk directly to that person; or the flak can decide – or find out – that the information sought is so sensitive that the question must be dealt with at a higher level. At that point it enters the realm of "politics," and the minister or deputy minister decides what to do next.

At times, an innocuous question will elicit a direct phone call from the minister responsible. When that happens, you're dealing with the most professional of the no-answer answerers, and you must be polite, and firm, and tenacious as a pit bull. If you have no success, don't stop yet.

The various commissars in charge of information might not want to tell you something, but there's a good chance that the piece of information has already entered the public realm in print. Vancouver *Sun* reporter Frances Bula, working the education beat, was surprised to learn that school districts throughout B.C. submit annual reports to the Ministry of Education. Those reports are made available to the public, and through them Bula was able to break a story on parents who were school-shopping around Vancouver, trying to enroll their kids in public schools the parents deemed were superior to their neighbourhood school. The practice of school shopping was quietly bringing grief to a lot of public schools, and Bula found the information she needed to write the story in an otherwise boring and tedious, fact-filled annual report.

Most ministries produce annual reports, as do larger government departments. They will never win prizes for literature, but they often contain fascinating facts and figures that will help your search. If you're not quite sure what you're looking for, a quick flip through the pages of the annual report for the department of interest might help you to formulate your question.

Unfortunately, there is no comprehensive directory of publications available from all B.C. government departments. Crown Publications Inc., the now-privatized company which sells publications produced by the Queen's Printer, prints a catalogue of certain government documents it has for sale, but the best way to find out what's available is to talk to the information officer, and to any helpful bureaucrats.

A publication available at your local library might also be helpful. Known as the *Microlog Index*, it is published by a Toronto company called Micromedia. It lists municipal, provincial and federal publications, along with publications of research associations, professional groups and special interest organizations.

Although most ministries adhere to policy guidelines when dealing with reporters and researchers, some helpful bureaucrats have been known to answer their own phones. And while they will rarely speak for the record, in fear of angering their political bosses, they will occasionally tell you what's available on public record so that you can look it up yourself. That's where the Government of B.C. Phone Directory comes in handy. It lists the names, numbers, and titles of all its bureaucrats.

Some information is readily available from the B.C. government without engaging in subterfuge and sweat. Government departments as varied as the ASSESSMENT AUTHORITY OF B.C. and the FIRE COMMISSIONER see their job as making information available to the public. The information they collect is helpful and readily available for the asking. Chapters scattered throughout this book explain how to ask, and what you might hope to find.

As a final resort against a stonewalling bureaucrat, the helpful folks in the offices of the provincial Ombudsman and the Auditor General will often direct you to the right piece of information. Your local MLA's office can also be helpful if you phone. And the Opposition's research department, located in Victoria, will sometimes lend a hand, particularly if the information you seek is potentially embarrassing to the government. Specialists in the field (see UNIVERSITIES, PROFESSIONAL ASSOCIATIONS) may also know of arcane government reports and records which may bear fruit.

To acquire a copy of the Government of British Columbia Phone Directory and a catalogue of B.C. government publications, write to:

Crown Publications
546 Yates Street
Victoria, B.C.
V8W IK8

BUSINESS LICENSES

THE PRO-CHOICE FORCES had been vowing for years to open a free-standing abortion clinic in Vancouver. They held fund-raisers, hired lawyers, held interminable news conferences to tell the public that opening day was just around the corner. Finally, in the winter of 1988, they said a building had been found. Expecting powerful opposition from "pro-life" advocates, the board of the abortion clinic decided to keep the location a secret until the clinic actually opened.

Members of the news media tried their best to ferret out the address, without success. But the pro-choicers had promised that everything they did would be legal and above-board. That meant they would have to apply for a business license. Any company or society doing business in a municipality in B.C. must obtain a license from the local municipal hall to run its operation. Licenses are a valuable source of revenue to municipal governments. More importantly, the permit system allows officials to ensure that private businesses live up to municipal standards affecting health, zoning, parking, and other neighbourhood concerns.

And, important to the researcher – municipal business licenses are open to public perusal. The information on the license includes the company's address, the type of business, and the names of company officials.

A worker with Vancouver city hall's business license office promised to let me know when a license had been granted to the abortion clinic. After some months, he was true to his word. He told me about the license, and I got the address. As it turned out, however, another reporter had been watching for the same thing. Holly Horwood from the Vancouver *Province* beat me to the story. Within hours of her exclusive report, reporters swarmed to the clinic offices on Victoria Drive in Vancouver to ask area residents if they feared trouble.

It's rare, of course, for the press to wait with bated breath for an organization to be granted a business license. And much of the information contained in the licenses often can be found – quicker and easier – in sources like CONTACTS INFLUENTIAL, CITY DIRECTORIES, and the REGISTRAR OF COMPANIES. But if an organization is operating in an area not covered by *Contacts* or the City Directory, the municipal hall's business license office is often the best place to start.

CANADIAN
ASSOCIATION
OF JOURNALISTS

THIS ORGANIZATION USED TO BE called the Centre for Investigative Journalism. Every time it advertised a seminar, members would get phone calls from people asking if the CIJ was connected to the CIA, and wondering what reporters were doing associating with the U.S. intelligence gathering service.

That was a minor drawback to the name. Detractors felt the term "investigative journalist" was elitist and arrogant, and kept some hard-working but humble prospective members from joining. The old name had its fans but, after years of wrangling, the members of the CIJ voted in June 1990 to change the name to the Canadian Association of Journalists (CAJ).

Whatever it's known as, the association is a loose-knit coalition of journalists – reporters, editors, publishers, researchers, academics – who want to do a better job of what they do. When the CIJ was founded in 1978, the initial members proposed that the goal of the organization be "to advance understanding of the concealed, obscure or complex aspects of matters that significantly affect the public."

The founders can be faulted for lofty ambitions, but their hearts were in the right place. There is no other association in Canada trying to improve the quality of journalism, and nowhere else for journalists or researchers to go to polish their craft. Aside from one paid staffer in Ottawa, the CAJ is run by volunteers, mostly reporters and editors who donate their time to set up regional and national seminars, contribute to the quarterly *CAJ Bulletin*, and answer questions from colleagues.

And that, perhaps, is its most important function. The CAJ is a network of interested newsies who will spend a few minutes to help a reporter from across town or across the country with an investigation. The CAJ network puts people in touch with each other to share information, research techniques, sources, and contacts. It's a valuable service, if everyone cooperates. The trouble, of course, is that reporters are like everyone else – jealous and proud of the tricks they've developed during the years, and sometimes unwilling to share those tricks with someone else. Despite the high-sounding prose of the CAJ goals, sometimes members are loathe to help out, so it might take a few phone calls to various reporters to find someone who is willing to lend a hand. Nevertheless, it is worthwhile.

The CAJ also publishes a directory of members and their interests, so if you're looking for someone who might be able to help out in an investigation on toxic wastes in tide water, or one on small-town public schools, the directory can save you some time.

As with any human endeavour, there's a cost involved. The CAJ charges annual members fees: $20 for students, $30 for people earning less than $20,000 a year, and $55 for anyone else. For that, you get the *Bulletin*, the membership directory, an annual collection of the best investigative journalism in print and broadcast, and reduced rates for seminars. It's not perfect, but the Canadian Association of Journalists is as close as Canada comes to anything which cares about the craft.

And, a note: despite the original name, there is no real "centre." The CAJ maintains an office in Ottawa, but most of the activities of the CAJ are handled by phone, or at meetings in coffee shops and bars.

The Canadian Association of Journalists
St. Patrick's Building
Room 324, Carleton University
Ottawa, Ont.
K1S 5B6
(613) 788-7424

CANADIAN
RADIO-TELEVISION &
TELECOMMUNICATIONS
COMMISSION (CRTC)

THE PEOPLE AT THE B.C. TRANSIT commission were not happy. They had been pressured to hire a consultant who had corporate connections to the minister responsible for transit – the minister who had "suggested" his hiring.

I was reporting for CBC Television News, working on a story about a cost overrun that B.C. Transit had suffered building a portion of SkyTrain in Vancouver. The person I was talking with didn't much want to discuss the SkyTrain budget. The information was touchy, it was a political hot potato, and any information would have to come from the politicians in charge – in this case, former cabinet minister Grace McCarthy.

But sometimes people don't like to see reporters leave empty-handed. Maybe they're generous, maybe they're media fans, maybe they're just plain odd. Whatever the case, the source at B.C. Transit wouldn't talk budgets, but he did hint at a totally unconnected story: some of his colleagues weren't pleased with the appointment of a Terrace businessman named J. Fred Weber, who was now on the public payroll. The source said that McCarthy had "strongly suggested" that Weber be hired as a consultant, and when your political master "suggests" that you jump, you answer, "How high?" The source also said that it was a well-known fact that Weber had business connections with the family of Grace McCarthy.

At least, that's what the source said. I knew that J. Fred Weber ran television station CFTK, the CBC affiliate in Terrace. But if he was connected to cabinet powerhouse McCarthy, it was news to me. The source at B.C. Transit didn't want to give any more information. He was worried that word might get back to McCarthy, and he'd be looking for work.

The Social Credit government had recently been shaken by a series of conflict of interest reports. A couple of ministers had been forced to resign in scandal, and no one in the public service wanted to anger their political masters by being publicly connected to another potential embarrassment for the provincial government. I was left with a couple of names, and what looked like a good tip.

And a good place to start. McCarthy's holdings were listed at the office of the Legislative Clerk in Victoria (see FINANCIAL DISCLOSURE ACT). Trouble was, politicians only have to reveal the bare minimum about their investments. Sure, McCarthy had revealed that she or her family had shares in companies called Grande Kalum Developments Co. Ltd., Aurora Enterprises Ltd., Hastings Properties Ltd. and Ray Danton Enterprises Ltd....but what the hell were those companies, and how did J. Fred Weber fit in?

A company search, set up by a telephone call (see REGISTRAR OF COMPANIES), determined that Weber was, in fact, one of two directors of the first company on the list – Grande Kalum Developments. The other director was Ray McCarthy, the husband of Grace McCarthy. So far, so good. The connection was proved...but a connection in what?

Next stop, the offices of the Canadian Radio-television and Telecommunications Commission. This is the federal watchdog body set up to oversee the public interest as it pertains to the granting of licenses to run television and radio stations. The CRTC is largely a toothless old dog; it often threatens to remove licenses if stations don't run up to snuff, but in fact has never lifted a single license. Nevertheless, the CRTC demands that licensees reveal all their corporate holdings to the commission. That meant that J. Fred Weber had to spill his financial guts into the files of the CRTC.

These financial statements are neatly tucked away into filing cabinets and largely forgotten, but they are open to anyone who wants to take a look. A helpful clerk at the CRTC office helped me find that Weber's corporate empire operated under the umbrella name of Skeena Broadcasters Ltd. Skeena's public disclosure revealed that Weber owned 50 percent of the shares of the company called Grande Kalum. In turn, Grande Kalum owned the building that housed Skeena's operations in the town of Terrace.

Skeena leased the building from Grande Kalum. So, in effect, J. Fred Weber paid his rent to himself. And to one other person: Ray McCarthy.

McCarthy confirmed in a telephone call to his home that he owned 50 percent of the shares of Grande Kalum, but he wouldn't say who owned the other half. However, the CRTC files had already revealed Weber's connection.

So Grace McCarthy had pressured B.C. Transit to put J. Fred Weber on the government payroll. This was the same J. Fred Weber who paid rent to McCarthy's husband. You might think this could be construed as something of a conflict of interest. You might think that. You would be wrong if you did.

"Of course we hire our friends," said a smiling Grace McCarthy. "We're not going to hire our enemies."

The story ran on the CBC TV News, including a segment in which a cameraman and I tried to interview J. Fred Weber as he got into his car on a Vancouver street and drove off, refusing to talk about his connection to McCarthy or SkyTrain. I would have liked to have seen the look on Weber's face that night. His station, CFTK, carried the CBC's *Night Final* newscast – the show that carried my story. And there, on the screens of the town of Terrace, was a picture of J. Fred Weber driving down the street, refusing to talk to the news media.

In Vancouver, the CRTC can be contacted at:

Canadian Radio-television and Telecommunications
  Commission
800 Burrard Street, Suite 1500
P.O. Box 1580
Vancouver, B.C.
V6Z 2G7
(604) 666-2111

CHARITIES

THE DIRECTORS OF CHILD FIND B.C. were justifiably indignant. People were phoning houses around B.C., seeking to raise money to help find missing children. The callers were suggesting that they were somehow connected to Child Find.

But the callers had no connection. People who thought they were donating money to Child Find were actually giving their hard-earned bucks to an Alberta-based telephone solicitation company. The issue of missing kids was a hot one in B.C., fueled by the memory of child-killer Clifford Olson's murderous rampage, and a recent Movie of the Week which had illustrated the epidemic of abducted children in the U.S. The directors of Vancouver-based Child Find were in a flap, and they contacted the media to spread the word that someone was using their name in vain. The story had broken in that morning's *Province*, and I was assigned to do a "matcher" – a news report basically covering ground that another reporter had already covered.

During the interview with Child Find, charity president Julie Cullen revealed that her organization was doubly incensed: Child Find had hired a fund-raiser of its own, another Alberta-based company which raised money for a fee. She was reluctant to reveal the exact cost, but then she let it slip: the company, Great West Entertainment, was giving the charity less than 10 cents for every dollar it raised. The bulk of the money was being spent covering the costs and profits of the corporate owners of Great West Entertainment.

That meant that people who thought they were donating money to charity were wrong. In fact, most of their money was going to a private, profit-making enterprise which had nothing to do with the issue of finding abducted children. Child Find finally severed its ties with Great West after its financial connection became known, but other charities continue using professional fund-raisers, and that means that a good percentage of the money you donate to a charitable cause never gets there.

Goods donated to the Vancouver Association for Mentally Handicapped People and to the Canadian Diabetes Association get sorted and sold through the chain of Value Village stores throughout B.C. Value Village is a California-based company with stores throughout the Pacific Northwest. For every dollar that Value Village raises, about ten cents goes to charity. Another Vancouver company, B&C Lists, regularly conducts telephone fund-raising campaigns on behalf of groups as diverse as sport clubs and hospitals. People who give their money to the clients of B&C Lists are told that the profits are split "80 percent to the charity, and 20 percent to us." That's true, as far as it goes. In the harsh light of economic reality, the 80-20 split is calculated after the overhead costs of B&C Lists are deducted. What's left over is usually just a few cents. And that means that just a few pennies for every dollar raised actually go to charity. The rest of the cash goes to B&C Lists, a private company controlled by the family of Vancouver businessman Jack Hyman.

Every charity suffers administration costs, of course. B.C.'s United Way campaign estimates that expenses such as advertising, special events, campaigns, and wages take up about 10 percent of the money it raises. The Heart Fund and Cancer Society's administrative costs take up about 14 percent of their donations. Those groups rely heavily on volunteers, and that's how they keep the costs down. The costs sky-rocket once a charity enters the realm of fund-raisers for hire.

There are no laws in B.C. regulating professional fund-raisers, or dictating how much money must go to charity. The City of Vancouver licensing department (see BUSINESS LICENSES) will not give a license to a fund-raising company that takes more than 20 percent of the money raised, but companies which get turned down for licenses quickly set up shop in unregulated suburbs and raise their funds and profits from there.

In short, no one is protecting you and your charitable dollar. The only way you can make sure that your money is going to charity is by demanding hard answers from the charity that's asking for your donation. Ask how much money actually goes to charity. If the answers are not convincing, ask yourself if your money might be better spent somewhere else.

If you're trying to find out who is behind a specific charity, remember that most charities in B.C. are operated by societies, and directors of those societies can be found through the REGIS-TRAR OF COMPANIES. As well, organizations doing charitable work in Canada must be granted a special tax-exempt status from Revenue Canada. The tax department maintains a special, toll-free line for anyone seeking information on whether or not a society is, in fact, a charity. Remember, though, that Ottawa has been accused of being lax in how it defines "charity." Groups such as the controversial Narconon program (see CULTS) and the big-business-funded Fraser Institute also have charitable tax status, so just because an organization has been recognized by Ottawa, it might not mean that you agree with the "charitable" aim of that particular group. Protect yourself and your money. No one else will.

Revenue Canada Charity Hot-Line:
1-800-267-2384

CITY DIRECTORIES
and CRISS-CROSS

NOTHING IS MORE IMPORTANT for tracking people down than city directories and criss-crosses. They are simple, fast, free of charge, and will save you time and sweat and tears. They are the most basic of the researcher's tools, because they list people and where to find them. One step up from the telephone book, the city directory is the first place to look.

Hunting for old neighbours of someone who has seemingly vanished off the face of the earth?

Searching for the address of someone who has an unlisted telephone number?

Got a phone number, but no name or address?

Take a look in the city directory or its companion volume, the criss-cross. Chances are good that your hunt might be finished within a few seconds.

City directories are published for 25 communities in B.C. Unlike the telephone books published by B.C. Tel, city directories are published by private companies. In this province, a company called B.C. Directories publishes the handy volumes.

Like the phone book, the city directory lists residents of a particular geographical area by last name, address, and phone number. But they also list occupations of the wage-earners living in that home. City directories also avoid the incipient sexism of telephone books by including the names of both spouses living in a particular home.

That extra bit of help can be invaluable.

For instance: you're looking for an accountant named Jane Smith who has diverted charitable funds to a number of politicians. The telephone book lists dozens of people named J. Smith. You could call them all, asking if this is the home of Jane Smith the accountant. But then you realize the fatal flaw of phone books – unless it is specially ordered, the phone company lists just one person: the so-called "man of the house," if there is one. You don't even know if Jane is married, never mind the name of her husband.

Hence, all the phone book can supply you with is the phone numbers of hundreds of Smiths. It would be cumbersome and time-consuming, to say the least, to phone them all. That's where the city directory comes in. A quick scan down the list of Smith, J, finds two Janes, but one is a mechanic and the other a lawyer. It takes a couple of minutes to read all the Smiths, but there, beside Smith, John, banker, is the name of his wife, Jane, and her occupation, accountant.

Smith, John, banker; Jane, acc't. 1234 Main Street, 555-1212.

Bingo. You've found her, with phone number and address.

But your hunt isn't over yet. You try the phone number and a recorded announcement tells you that the phone number is no longer in service.

"Damn!" you say. They've moved. But it ain't necessarily so.

The city directory is divided into two sections. The first lists people by last names. The second section lists people by their street address. Turn to the second section. The pages for Main Street list the occupants, by house and/or apartment number, of every adult living on the street. By using the directory, you can quickly find Jane's neighbours – at 1232 and 1236 Main Street. Phone them, and ask where you can find Jane. Chances are good they'll know where she's gone. Or the neighbours will tell you that no one has moved out of Jane Smith's house. That means the Smiths have changed their phone number, but are still living at the same address. You have the house number, so all you have to do is pay the Smiths a visit.

This also works for people who vanished off the face of the earth years earlier. Before they became important – and hidden – they were likely listed in their local city directory. And they had neighbours. And neighbours often stay in touch.

On rare occasions, you'll wind up with a telephone number, but no name, and no address. The operator (see DIRECTORY ASSISTANCE) at B.C. Tel is under corporate instructions not to divulge the owner of a specific phone number. But the directory called criss-cross (also known as the "phone locator") lists home addresses for telephone numbers. The front section of the book runs down all the telephone numbers for its area in numerical order. If you had the Smiths' phone number, 555-1212, a scan down the page of the criss-cross would inform you that the phone number was registered to the home at 1234 Main Street. The criss-cross also has a street number section, so a quick flip to the back of the book would tell you that 1234 Main Street was registered as the home of John and Jane Smith.

Of course, people who want to stay hidden often decline to register with the city directory, but you will be surprised at how many otherwise unreachable people can be found in your local directory. Prices for the directories range from $85-$95 for smaller communities, up to $300 and more for Greater Vancouver. But you can also find city directories free of charge in most local public libraries.

In B.C., city directories are published for the communities of Abbotsford-Clearbrook, Campbell River, Chilliwack, Courtenay-Comox, Cranbrook-Kimberley, Dawson Creek, Duncan, Fort St. John, Kamloops, Kelowna, Nanaimo, Nelson, Penticton, Port Alberni, Powell River, Prince George, Prince Rupert, Quesnel, Terrace-Kitimat, Trail-Rossland, Vernon, Victoria, Williams Lake, and, of course, Greater Vancouver, including the suburbs. Unfortunately, criss-crosses are published only for Greater Vancouver and the Greater Victoria area.

COMPETITORS

THERE IS NOTHING uniquely British Columbian about using competitors to snoop into the activities of a company or individual. It's a basic law of capitalism that opposing forces know each other's business. And as a result of the profit motive, the competition is often eager to share that information with people raking muck.

It is the business of businesses to mind their own business – and to keep tabs on the business of competitors. Corporations have to be aware of what the other guy is up to, so they can move first, buy first, sell first, do whatever it takes to beat the competition and make money. Whether you're looking into a possible consumer scam or an industry suspected of dumping toxic wastes into your back yard, you can be certain of one thing: if anyone knows the truth, or the dirt, it's the person who is competing with the suspect target.

A smart business person knows what services the competition offers, what ingredients they use, what technical processes are involved, and what regulations must be followed. And if there's anything in it for him or her to gain by sharing that information, they will.

So if you're starting off cold, investigating a company or service, talk to someone in a similar business. Be honest with the source. Tell them what you're looking for, and ask for suggestions on how to find it. Usually, conversations like these are conducted quietly (see BACKGROUND and OFF THE RECORD), but they are a good place to start. Business people who otherwise wouldn't give a nosy researcher the time of day are often more than happy to dump on the competition. That means that anything they say *must* be confirmed by official sources, but when you're looking for leads to follow, the competitors will usually provide you with industry gossip and inside information.

As for finding the competition, it's as easy as letting your fingers take a walk through the Yellow Pages or CONTACTS INFLUENTIAL. Locate a company which advertises in the same section as the company you're investigating, and give them a call.

Working the competition is also effective with politicians. Members of opposing political parties are more than happy to help dig dirt on their political foes, and will sometimes use their own contacts to help an inquiring mind. And remember that members of the same political party are also in competition with each other. They compete for chairmanships, for perks and press, for cabinet seats and the ear of their political leader. Politicians often have something to gain if a member of their own party takes a dive, and the concept of political solidarity falls to pieces when a hungry politician sees the chance to move up a notch and defeat a rival. You don't want to tip your hand to the person you're investigating, but if you've made a good contact on a municipal council, at city hall, or in the Legislative Assembly, and can trust that source not to reveal your inquiries, a quiet question often elicits a helpful response.

COMPUTER DATABASES

THE REPORTER WAS SERIOUS, imperious, and demanding, as only reporters on an important story can be. He strode to the news librarian's desk and said, "Give me everything the *Sun's* done on salmon."

"Everything?" asked the librarian.

"Yep. Everything," the reporter said.

Now, anyone who's read the Vancouver *Sun* knows the paper does a lot of stories on fish, a lot of stories on salmon. Probably more than 5000 since the paper's stories started being stored on computer in 1987. The librarian knew the reporter didn't want "everything." Printing out every story that contained the word "salmon" would take hours of computer time and cost hundreds, maybe thousands, of dollars. To comply with the request would mean the librarian would wind up dumping a metre-high stack of computer printout on the reporter's desk later in the day, and the reporter would mumble and curse that the bloody librarians were wasting his time.

The librarian knew that she'd have to narrow the search down.

"Does that mean you want the recipes too?" she asked, recalling the paper's food pages had run countless salmon recipes over the years.

"Hell no," harrumphed the reporter.

It was only then that the reporter finally opened up and told the librarian what, in fact, he was looking for. The Supreme Court of Canada had just handed down an important decision on a native Indian fishery case, and he wanted the news stories that pertained to that court battle. The librarian was able to tell the computer to search for stories which mentioned the name of the native involved and the word "salmon." Instead of thousands of stories, the computer narrowed the list down to less than a dozen. Total search time: a few minutes. Total cost on the computer: a few dollars.

And that's the secret to successful searches through computer databases – make the search as tight as possible so you don't waste time and money uncovering data that is useless but expensive.

Even with the narrowest of searches, though, computer databases can still burn a deep hole in your expense account. Fees can vary from $8 an hour to $8 a minute, depending on the database used. Then there are long-distance calling rates, first-time hookup charges, and extra billing for documents you look at along the way.

Sometimes a computer is the only way to go. When Ferdinand Marcos fled the Phillipines amid reports that he and his colleagues had sucked the national treasury dry, some of his cronies wound up in B.C. Reporters in Vancouver punched the names of these cronies into the data banks of U.S. newspapers. It was basically a fishing expedition to see if there was a Vancouver connection to any of the money. There was. Some of Vancouver's Filipino businessmen had been mentioned in U.S. papers from Los Angeles to Boston as they were buying properties and getting involved in lawsuits.

The Vancouver reporters had their hook, and just had to pay for a couple of long-distance phone calls to verify the U.S. reports.

Closer to home, researchers trying to pin down information on weekends, when government offices are closed, used to have to bite their nails until Monday morning. Now they can use the BC OnLine computer database for information about companies, societies, and land (see ASSESSMENT AUTHORITY OF B.C. and LAND TITLES).

But many researchers are falling into the trap of relying solely on computers and forsaking paper files. That's a big mistake. Databases can help you find what you're looking for, if you know what you're looking for. But paper files, compiled by real live humans with all their eccentricities and eclecticism, often contain bits of paper and wisdom that the researcher never knew existed. Ruffling through the kinds of paper files maintained in public libraries, for instance, or the Better Business Bureau, inquisitive researchers know they're looking for something to find, and they don't dismiss the odds and ends of material clipped from obscure publications just because they've never heard of the information or publication.

There's another plus to most paper files: they're free.

Nevertheless, the computer database business is booming, and more and more information sources are being pulled out of filing cabinets and punched into data retrieval systems. Below are a few computer databases that anyone with a personal computer and a modem – and the cash to pay the bills – can use to find information by and about British Columbians and things affecting B.C.

BC OnLine (1-800-663-6102)

At $7 and hour and $5 a search, this is one of the cheapest computer data bases available to researchers. BC OnLine offers access to records about companies, societies, land titles, and liens against motor vehicles. It's primarily designed for lawyers and real estate agents, but can be helpful to researchers, mostly because of its operating hours: 8 a.m. to 8 p.m., Monday through Saturday. The information contained in BC OnLine is available for free through other methods, but people in a hurry might find it useful. Researchers unwilling to sign up will also find there are BC OnLine customers in their towns already, who might grant them access to the services.

Infomart Online (in Vancouver: (604) 433-6125; elsewhere: 1-800-268-7742)

Southam Inc. owns most of Canada's major daily papers – including the Vancouver *Sun* and *Province* – and now offers the stories from those papers on computer database. The system also gives users access to the Canadian Press wire service database, magazines like the *Northern Miner* and *Maclean's*, and U.S. papers from the Seattle *Times* to the Washington *Post*. By the summer of 1990 it was charging customers $175 to hook up, and fees from $1.71 a minute to $3.96 a minute, depending on the time of day and the database selected. A reminder to researchers short on cash: some of the same information can be garnered for free from local public libraries.

Info Globe (Vancouver: (604) 685-1402; elsewhere: 1-800-268-9128)

The *Globe and Mail*, the Torontocentric "national newspaper," has some of the country's best reporters working on issues affecting the whole of Canada. As befits a service originating in a self-described "world-class city," Info Globe's prices are world-class too: in the summer of 1990 users faced a $399 hook-up charge, and search rates of $3.60 a minute in prime time. The *Globe and Mail* offers its own stories, corporate information, the *Canadian Periodical Index*, and access to government documents.

CONTACTS INFLUENTIAL

ON A RECENT EPISODE of *Jake and the Fatman*, an anguished Jake implores a fellow investigator to track down the owner of a company whose business card has been found in the pockets of a murder victim. The business card is the key, and if Jake can only find out who runs the business, he can find the witness and solve the crime. On television, the search takes hours and is completed barely in time for the last commercial.

But that's television, in a series filmed in Hawaii. If Jake's search had taken place in B.C., he would have had plenty of time to solve the crime. Jake would have opened the pages of a volume called *Contacts Influential* and found his answer in seconds, leaving plenty of time to add a couple of car chases and a shoot-out to the last half of his show. He might have even gotten the girl.

Contacts Influential is a book published for sales people, the business equivalent of the city directory. It lists the names of every business operation in the Lower Mainland – 44,000 in the 1989 Vancouver volume. As well as business names and addresses and phone numbers, *Contacts* also includes the names of the top two people in the company, usually the president and vice-president. A chapter at the back of the book called the "Key Individuals Section" lists the company brass in alphabetical order. The book is designed to help sales people contact the important people in any given company, either by telephone or direct mail. But the book is also a boon to researchers.

Got a name, but no idea where the person works? If the person you're seeking holds an important role in a company, you'll find them in the Key Individuals Section.

Trying to surreptitiously check out a company to find out who runs it? Flip open the book to the first chapter, and you'll find the company officers listed.

Contacts Influential is a particular life-saver to researchers working on weekends and nights, when no one is answering the phone at company search in Victoria (see **REGISTRAR OF COMPANIES**). I've lost count of the times that a company has been involved in a disaster or tragedy – air crashes, mining deaths, toxic spills, arson – and newsrooms have scrambled looking for a company official to comment. Usually, the search can be solved in a few seconds. First use *Contacts Influential* to determine the names of the company officers. Then use the city directory (see **CITY DIRECTORIES AND CRISS-CROSS**) to find the home phone numbers for those officials.

During the day, even when the Registrar of Companies is available, *Contacts Influential* is also handy to look up the name of a company president involved in a matter that you're researching. That way, when you phone the company, you can ask for the top person by name, and avoid being hindered by secretaries and low-level bureaucrats who feel their job is to protect the boss.

Contacts Influential is published by a company called Contacts Target Marketing Inc. There are separate volumes published for the Lower Mainland and for Greater Victoria (10,000 businesses.) Unfortunately, the rest of B.C. is not yet covered. It's an expensive proposition to own the book – $635 for the Lower Mainland edition, $349 for Victoria – but most libraries stock their own copy of *Contacts Influential*, so you can use it for free.

An important note to journalists: *Contacts Influential* is published annually, so some of the information it contains might be out of date by the time you use it. To avoid lawsuits or mistakes, it is important to confirm a person's connection to a business before reporting it, either with the person or company involved, or with the Registrar of Companies. Presidents and vice-presidents change jobs, and the top officer you're looking for might no longer be connected to the firm mentioned in *Contacts Influential*.

Contacts Target Marketing Inc.
1266 East Georgia Street
Vancouver, B.C.
V6A 2B1
(604) 253-1111

CORONERS

"I DON'T THINK THAT AIDS is a thing that should worry the gay public."

It was April 1983, and the speaker was Dr. Donald Huggins, a consultant to the Vancouver city health department. The disease called Acquired Immune Deficiency Syndrome was new, mysterious, and largely unknown. Huggins didn't think it was much of a big deal. He warned that homosexuals should be more concerned about a rise in syphilis and other sexually transmitted diseases.

Despite the doctor's best intentions, the gay network in Vancouver was worried. City doctors were already examining gay men, spurred on by reports from the World Health Organization in Geneva which warned that this new disease was on the rise. In the city, an organization called AIDS Vancouver had been formed to educate and spread the word that sexual contact might have something to do with the disease.

Dr. Huggins didn't know it, but two men had already died of AIDS in Vancouver (see ALTERNATIVE PRESS). Word of the deaths hadn't been made public. A member of AIDS Vancouver gave me the name of a city doctor who was participating in the study, and the doctor revealed the deaths to me. But the doctor was worried about a public backlash, a panic. He demanded that his identity be kept a secret, and would not reveal the identities of the victims. The doctors were nervous, fearing an increase in homophobia. Their research was medical, scientific, not for public consumption.

Inquiries around Canada revealed that the Red Cross in Toronto was already asking members of the homosexual population to refrain from donating blood. In B.C., there was no such policy. It wasn't until I contacted the B.C. and Yukon Red Cross – the organization which collects blood donations for the provincial health ministry – that a director noted it might be a good idea if homosexuals and intravenous drug users abstained from donating blood. A couple of years later it would be learned that hundreds of people had been infected with the deadly virus from contaminated blood products.

But this was 1983, and the official medical community did not appear overly worried. Still, this peculiar disease seemed important to some members of the community, and looked like a story that might not go away. I set out to find more, but the doctors dealing with the disease weren't talking. Their medical records were confidential and they wouldn't help in putting a human face to the disease.

However, doctors aren't the only people who keep records. The B.C. Coroners Service is charged with the duty, under law, to find out why people died, and to suggest methods of preventing future deaths. Former Vancouver coroner Glen McDonald used to call himself "ombudsman for the dead." Neither doctors nor the B.C. Ministry of Health would release any information on victims of AIDS, but the B.C. Coroners Service readily agreed to share its information because that's what it is legislated to do – find ways of averting death.

As it turned out, the Coroners Service had been called to investigate a sudden death the previous month. The official Coroner's Report of Inquiry, available to the public, said that a 28-year-old man named Mark Minogue had died at home, alone. Police were called to his West End apartment building when a tenant reported water leaking from a cupboard in his kitchen. The building manager checked for the source of the water and found Mark Minogue lying face down on the kitchen floor with water overflowing from the sink.

Coroner Val Steggles interviewed people who knew Minogue, and found that he was homosexual and had been complaining of a cough and general poor health in his last few days. An autopsy showed a disease called *pneumocystis carinii* pneumonia, a relatively rare illness that had been showing up in victims of AIDS. It's likely that Mark Minogue didn't even know the name of the disease that finally killed him. The coroner's report helped to bring the reality of AIDS to the public's attention, and publicized the importance of abstaining from risky sexual involvement. The coroner also recommended that people in the AIDS risk groups refrain from donating blood.

In San Francisco, Mark Minogue's father hadn't known what killed his son. In Vancouver, thanks to the coroner's report, people started talking, and thinking, about this bizarre new disease with the peculiar acronym which would soon be embedded in the public's consciousness.

The B.C. Coroners Service has regional offices throughout the province. They're listed in the telephone book blue pages.

COURTS

WE MET VANCOUVER BUSINESSMAN Joe Hargitt in the section on the Better Business Bureau. A lot of investors wish they had met him in that chapter, too – met him, that is, before they gave money to Hargitt. It might have saved them some grief.

By the time I met one of the investors, a Vancouver contractor, he had hired a private investigator in hopes of uncovering some dirt to help him recover the $25,000 he had invested in Hargitt's "company." The PI charged several hundred dollars to do what any inquisitive investigator can do for free: he visited the registry of the Supreme Court in Vancouver and scoured the civil court indexes to see if anyone had ever issued a civil lawsuit against Joe Hargitt. More than half a dozen had, the investigator found, listing the same complaint in their legal documents: that Hargitt had sold them a piece of a company with no assets.

The investor wished he had taken a look through the court files before he invested money.

You don't have to be a PI or have a law degree to work your way through court registries. They're about as difficult as the Yellow Pages, and often a lot more illuminating. Trouble is, too many people are intimidated by the courts to think of doing it themselves. That fear is propagated by lawyers eager to increase their billing hours, and by private investigators unwilling to share their techniques. Later in this chapter we'll meet some lawyers willing to give members of the public a hand through the legal system, but for now, a quick primer on that system.

The handbook of the **INVESTIGATIVE REPORTERS AND EDITORS, INC.** notes that most veteran reporters and researchers have less legal knowledge than the average second-year law student. (As assignment editor with CBC TV News in Vancouver, I remember listening to a counterpart at an affiliate in the north tell me that he had a rule of thumb for his reporters: don't cover the courts. Ever. That way, he reasoned, they'd never get anything wrong.)

One thin chapter in a thin book isn't going to make you a legal expert, but it will help take some of the mystery out of the ways B.C. courts store their information.

Let's look at the case of Joe Hargitt. Anyone suspicious of our friend Joe, if they thought about it, would have reason to wonder if he had ever been sued. That is, if anyone had ever asked a civil court judge to listen to both sides of the argument and rule if the money had been properly handled. It's a reasonable thing to wonder about. Where do you go from there?

First, understand that the courts in B.C. are divided into several different sections. Crimes against the Criminal Code of Canada – from drug possession to bank robbery to murder – are heard in the Provincial and Supreme Courts. In these matters, the police are involved. They gather information and present their findings to Crown Counsel, the lawyers acting for the provincial Attorney General's department. If those lawyers determine that a crime has been commited, the matter is heard in a court of law, either before a judge alone or a judge and jury.

The background and files collected in those cases are held by the court registry and are not available to the public. However, members of the public are granted access to the written decisions of judges, which often contain the important background details of the case. Also confidential are records of things the court deems are family matters, including divorces and cases involving juveniles.

But when it comes to money and property, the courts of B.C. feel we deserve access to the records. In civil cases, in which one person sues another and there is no police involvement, the records are retained by the court and are available for perusal by anyone who asks. All you have to do is think of asking, and visit the courts in person.

Court registries keep a binder of civil cases in a public spot at the local courthouse. Larger courts, like the Supreme Court in Robson Square in downtown Vancouver, produce computerized lists in alphabetical order, listing the names of the plaintiff and defendant – the person who's suing and the person being sued. Smaller registries often handwrite the names in a ledger. All you have to do is pore through the directories, known as indexes among court registrars, until you find the name you're looking for. Beside the names is the File Number issued to the particular case. Give the registrar the file number, and the registrar will hunt around the stacks of files until the one you want is found. Then it's happy reading.

There's something else you've got to know: civil cases involving money are heard in different courts. If the matter in dispute is worth less than $3,000, that case is heard in Small Claims Court, a division of the Provincial Court. (At the time of writing the sum was expected to increase to $5,000.) Those files are kept in the Provincial Court registry.

If the sum involved is more than $3,000 (expected to increase to more than $5,000), the matter is dealt with in the Supreme Court, and the Supreme Court registry will have the files you're looking for. As well, at the time of this writing the government was expected to introduce a system of "economic litigation" cases for sums between $5,000 and $20,000, so you might have to look through three different registries to find the case you're looking for.

Fortunately, the vast majority of court registries in B.C. are unified. That means the registries handle everything, from provincial to small claims to Supreme. If you don't know how to find what you're looking for, ask the registrar for a hand.

Unfortunately, for our purposes, registries don't talk to each other, and there are more than 50 scattered throughout B.C. So if Joe Hargitt gets sued in Surrey, there's no mention of it in the Vancouver court registry. Persistent researchers must visit all the registries that might be involved, until they find what they're looking for. The courts plan to computerize their files so all civil matters are available from a central registry, but that process is expected to take until 1995 to complete.

For the location of the court registry in your area, look in the blue pages of your telephone book under: Government of B.C.: Court Services section, Court Registries.

And you don't need a Joe Hargitt in your community to find the courts a worthwhile source of information. Several community newspapers visit their courthouses for a regular poke through the files to run a column called "Who's Suing Who?" which is invariably one of the best-read sections of the paper in this increasingly litigious society.

If, however, you're like the CBC assignment editor who had a blanket ban on the courts because they were just too mystifying, you might need a hand. The Attorney General's department is opening five regional offices of the Law Courts Education Society in B.C., providing staff whose job it is to help you figure out how the courts work. If you don't think you can go it alone, try them.

Law Courts Education Society:

Lower Mainland West
219-800 Smithe Street
Vancouver, B.C.
V6Z 2E1
(604) 660-2919

Lower Mainland (East Region) (after October 1, 1990)
c/o Surrey Courthouse
14245-56th Avenue
Surrey, B.C.
V3W 1J2

Interior
The Kamloops Law Courts
Room 405A, 455 Columbia Street
Kamloops, B.C.
V2C 2T3
(604) 828-4662

Northern
Prince George Court Services
3rd Floor, 1600 Third Avenue
Prince George, B.C.
V2L 3G6
(604) 565-6075

Vancouver Island (after April 1, 1991)
Victoria Law Courts
850 Burdett Avenue
Victoria, B.C.
V8W 1B4
(604) 356-1478

Fraser Valley
New Westminster Law Courts
Begbie Square
New Westminster, B.C.
(604) 660-8522

If you're a reporter working on a court case, one of the lawyers involved in the case will usually provide any assistance you need in ensuring the case gets covered accurately and fairly. For other people looking into legal matters, a quick chat with a friendly lawyer might be worthwhile. The Legal Services Society provides a lawyer referral service, in which you can discuss your problem with a lawyer for up to 30 minutes for a fee of $10. There are 50 offices around B.C. Again, look in your phone book under Legal Services Society for the office nearest you.

CULTS

THE TIP CAME FROM A FRIEND of a friend of a friend: members of the Church of Scientology were distributing literature at day-care centres in Burnaby. I knew as much about Scientology as the next guy. It had been created by a former writer of science fiction novels, it was an international organization, it had come into questionable repute during the years, adherents were vocal, and Scientologists had a penchant for suing reporters who had the temerity to poke around the doings of the so-called "church."

And now some day-care operators were upset that Scientologists had distributed literature without revealing their connection to the controversial organization. In fact, they had visited the day cares calling themselves members of "The Concerned Businessman's Association." On its own, it didn't mean much...a couple of visits, a peculiar name. But if Scientologists were operating under another name, might they be involved in other activities, using other names?

That was the question that came to mind. The answer wasn't so easy. The tip had come from a former member of Scientology, a high-ranking officer who had defected from the organization several years earlier, carrying with her some internal Scientology documents. Those papers offered me the first look inside the organization. The public face of the Church of Scientology is a group of well-dressed young people eager to offer "free personality tests," gain recruits, and make the world a better place. Ottawa has recognized that face – some of the organizations operated by members of the church have been granted charitable tax status (see CHARITIES) by the federal government.

There was precious little information available on Scientology from the regular sources – library files, newspaper morgues, court records. Cults have a habit of suing anyone who starts looking around into their activities, and in today's climate of libel chill, most newsrooms are loathe to initiate stories which will likely wind up in the courts, no matter how trivial or vexatious the lawsuit. It's been more than 10 years since 900 people committed suicide at the urging of cult leader Jim Jones in Guyana, but there is still no governmental or religious body studying cults, no central registry of information to help the public assess these organizations.

A lot of phone calls later, I stumbled onto an international network of cult-watchers, specialists in the doings of organizations such as the Church of Scientology. In fact, several of the groups are headed by former members of Scientology, people who are eager to warn others of the dangers of mind control. Working alone, or in small groups, these people have assembled vast collections of documents, background papers, and analyses of hundreds of cults worldwide.

In Calgary, former Scientologist Brendan Moore operates what he calls the Cult Information Service, a private association monitoring and studying the activities of various organizations, collecting background on the cults and their leaders and, most importantly, their recruiting methods. (Unfortunately, there is no cult-watching group in B.C., but groups outside the province are more than willing to lend a hand.) It was Moore who gave me a thick stack of background on Scientology, including a number of internal Scientology documents, which indicated names that Scientologists had used previously in other cities, in other times. Names like Parents Interested in Education. The Citizens Commission on Human Rights. Effective Education Schools. Narconon.

Once I had the names that Scientology had used, it was simple to check society records in Victoria (see REGISTRAR OF COMPANIES) to see if there were similar organizations operating in B.C. There were. And by cross-checking names of society directors, I was able to link the various groups to the Church of Scientology's head office. Those names led to other names, and a pattern emerged... a pattern which indicated that Scientologists were recruiting and raising money under a host of names.

Moore's affiliates in England also provided me with a judgment of the High Court of London, in which a judge had labeled Scientology a "sinister and dangerous cult." The judge further stated that the practices of Scientology are "immoral and socially obnoxious." That judgment was instrumental in getting the story to air. The Scientologists had threatened a lawsuit early on in my investigation, ensuring that anything I proposed to report would be scrupulously examined by CBC lawyers. The opinion of any cult watcher – no matter how "expert" that opinion may be – would be subject to a challenge if the matter ever got into a court of law. But decisions by judges are privileged (see COURTS), which meant that I could use the comments of the British judge in my reports on the activities of Scientology, even though those comments had been made thousands of kilometres away.

Hence, the CBC carried my reports, revealing that Scientologists were actively recruiting members and raising money under a plethora of names. They were operating day-care centres for toddlers, and private schools and tutors for kids, without pointing out to unsuspecting parents that their children would be exposed to teaching techniques that the London judge had said would "indoctrinate them so that they become unquestioning captives and tools of the cult...."

Scientologists didn't like my reports. Coincidentally, the stories ran in the middle of a direct-mail campaign in which the "Narconon" program asked B.C. residents to donate money to Narconon – a request that was made without pointing out the connection of Narconon to the Church of Scientology. The City of Vancouver, however, took interest in the reports. City hall advised the B.C. Assessment Authority to re-examine the church's tax-exempt headquarters in downtown Vancouver. Now the B.C. government has told Scientology that it will have to start paying taxes on its building, because the headquarters are used less for the practice of religion and more for the making of money.

Cult contacts:

Brendan Moore
Cult Information Service
#514, 209-8th Ave., S.W.
Calgary, Alta.
T2P 1B8
(403) 261-6754

Council on Mind Abuse
Robert Tucker
Suite 203, 40 St. Clair Avenue East
Toronto, Ont.
M4T 1M9
(416) 944-0080

Cult Project
3460 Stanley Street
Montreal, PQ
H3A 1R8
(514) 845-9171

Cult Awareness Network *(publishes monthly newsletter)*
2421 West Pratt Blvd. Suite 1173
Chicago, Illinois 60645
(312) 267-7777

DIRECTORY ASSISTANCE

CLARK WINTERTON was a macho cop with a closet full of commendations. He was also the son of Don Winterton, the former chief of the Vancouver police department. That's why it seemed so strange when Clark Winterton willingly handed in his badge and resigned from the force in 1986. The career constable had been the subject of a secret, internal police inquiry, and had been suspended earlier that year. The current police chief, Bob Stewart, would only say that Winterton had resigned, and that his resignation concerned the constable's conduct during a burglary investigation sometime that year.

For Stewart, the matter was finished. The resignation, said the chief, "negates any internal discipline proceedings stemming from an inquiry into his behavior."

That might have been good enough for the chief of police, but it wasn't good enough for BCTV reporter John L. Daly. Why would a cop suddenly pack it in? he wondered. There was obviously more to the story than a matter of "behaviour" or a bad attitude. A constable with 11 years on the force doesn't suddenly decide to quit his job unless he's been caught doing something he shouldn't have done. Daly started poking around.

This would be no easy investigation. Under the B.C. Police Act, complaints about city police are investigated by the police department itself – the police, policing the police. Inquiries are held internally, secretly, and the public is rarely told what goes on behind those closed doors. And cops tend to keep things to themselves...particularly things that make them look bad.

But although cops wouldn't talk to him, Daly knew that someone, somewhere, would have the details of the story. He started off cold, phoning everyone he could think of, to try to find out what was going on. He scoured the daily reports of the Vancouver city police – those reports are open to the public – looking for a report with Winterton's name on it. Daly knew that Winterton's beat covered the wealthy Vancouver neighbourhood of Shaughnessy, so he paid particular attention to reports covering crime activity in that area.

He came up dry. The files contained nothing that might point to Winterton's involvement in any wrongdoing. Daly didn't know where else to turn. So he did what any other good researcher should do: he asked the guy at the next desk. As it turned out, that person happened to be a beginning journalist working for free as a researcher, hoping to break into the business. No matter how inexperienced freshman journalists might be, one thing is certain – they have friends and family, and those people have friends and family. And people gossip.

The researcher had heard some gossip to the effect that Winterton had been forced to resign, something to do with a piece of jewelry, perhaps a ring. There was something else. One of the people involved was an avid golfer.

No names, no places, no dates. Nowhere else to turn. Daly went home, exhausted, pissed off. He didn't have much to go on. A ring. Golf. Sitting on the couch, Daly remembered a woman he had taught once in a journalism course, a woman with a fanatic interest in the game of golf. On a whim, on a hunch, Daly phoned the woman.

And the woman had heard the story. It had made the rounds of the city's more exclusive golf courses. A retired lumberman named John Fairburn was involved. Trouble is, said the woman, Fairburn was nowhere to be found. He spent half the year somewhere in Arizona, and was there now. And that was that. Daly now had a name, but precious little else. A visit to the Vancouver Public Library's main branch unearthed one small newspaper clipping with Fairburn's name, but no indication of where the elusive man might be found. Daly went back to the BCTV newsroom and, again on a hunch, he got the area code for the state of Arizona and phoned directory assistance.

It's a funny thing about wealthy people. They usually remain hidden and secretive at home, with unlisted phone numbers and tight-lipped friends. But when they relax at winter retreats in the southern states, they'll often allow themselves to be listed in the local telephone book in case their wealthy friends want to call. (It's important to note that just because someone isn't in the telephone book, it doesn't mean they're unlisted and not findable. It might mean they've acquired their phone number recently and are not yet published in the telephone directory. Take a few seconds to phone the directory assistance operator to ask if the phone number is available.)

The state of Arizona has only three major population centres, and the operator checked first for Yuma. There was a listing for a Fairburn, John. Daly called the number, asking if this was the home of John Fairburn from Vancouver. It was.

Fairburn readily agreed to talk. He told Daly that his Vancouver home had been robbed the previous year. Constable Winterton had visited the home to investigate. The strangest thing had happened. Fairburn's wife was sure that her $60,000 emerald ring hadn't been taken in the robbery. It was still sitting in her jewelry box. But after Winterton left, she checked again and the ring was gone.

The Fairburns told Winterton about the ring, and the policeman told the family that he would check with his contacts in the criminal underworld. Winterton contacted the family a while later, telling them he had a lead on the ring from one of his contacts and could get it back for a $6,000 reward.

The Fairburns gave Winterton the cash, and the cop gave them the ring. But John Fairburn didn't figure the episode smelled right. He complained to the city police department, which investigated the story. A chastened Winterton later returned the money to the Fairburns and resigned from the force.

The matter would have ended there, if not for Daly's television reports of the story. The rest of the media picked up on what seemed to be a gross injustice – why do ordinary thieves go to jail when they're caught, while thieves who happen to be police officers do not go to jail? Attorney General Brian Smith investigated, and Winterton was subsequently charged. The cop was finally sentenced to four months in jail after pleading guilty to theft. Daly won that year's award for B.C.'s top news story from the Jack Webster Foundation.

DUMPSTER DIVING

IT WAS A CASUAL telephone tip that turned Nicole Parton on to a story exposing the Vancouver connection to a consumer scam dubbed "the most sophisticated pyramid scheme of the 1980s." During her days on the consumer beat at the Vancouver *Sun*, Parton received dozens of phones calls a day, asking for advice and suggesting stories. There wasn't enough time in the day to follow every lead, but this tip seemed particularly interesting. Potential investors in a bizarre pyramid scheme were being told they could receive profits as high as 318 percent on their initial investment.

If there's one thing any wise consumer knows, it's this: the only thing you get for nothing is nothing. Unfortunately, there are unwise consumers born every minute, and despite countless warnings urging buyers to beware, there are con artists who understand that some people can be fooled...and foolish. Parton's tipster also provided her with a tantalizing carrot – newspaper clippings which exposed a similar scam in other countries. In the U.S., court cases had dealt with complaints that 30,000 investors in 22 states had been fleeced of about $100 million. Those court cases happened after the investors had lost their money. Now, Parton was told, the same scam had just moved into B.C. and was setting up shop.

Under the scheme, investors were sold small envelopes of skim milk powder mixed with lactobacillus culture. They were told to mix the stuff with milk and store it in a drinking glass. A yogurt-like culture grew on top of the glass after a week. That was skimmed off, put into envelopes, and dried. The investors were told there was a huge demand for the culture, that it was used in cosmetics, sports medicine, even cancer drugs. They were told that a company in Winnipeg would purchase the milk cultures and send them cheques. The profit-making capacity was amazing, said the people behind the scheme.

U.S. law officials were a tad more skeptical. The capacity for people to be unsuspecting was amazing, they had found. Several states had already ruled that the scheme was an illegal "Ponzi" scheme – named after a 1920s conman named Charles Ponzi – and that most of the dried milk cultures were merely sold to other investors. It was a pyramid scheme, which only works for as long as new investors can be found to pay earlier investors. The trouble with pyramid-investment schemes is that they inevitably collapse under their own weight. The first people in the scheme make money, but those who invest later get left holding the bag or, in this case, the glass of sour milk.

An intriguing story, and an important one. Because the scheme had just started in B.C., a news report uncovering the scheme could actually save people money by alerting possible victims before they invested. But where to begin? Fortunately, the newspaper clippings provided the names of companies which had been formed in the U.S. to manage the scheme, and Parton quickly determined that similar companies with similar names were already doing business in B.C. (see REGISTRAR OF COMPANIES). The clippings also noted that the scheme had its roots in South Africa and Indonesia. This was no local scam. Parton soon amassed a desk-full of information, and realized that she was getting bogged down. She asked the newspaper's city desk for help, and reporter Brian Power was assigned to work with Parton on the story.

Power, now working in Hong Kong, was renowned in the newsroom for being methodical, meticulous, and thorough. He had learned the secret of keeping things straight:

- Keep notes in separate file folders;
- Date notes;
- Use a separate sheet of paper for each interview;
- Keep immaculate notes and records of conversations so you can understand them and review them a year or two later if some-one sues and the case goes to trial.

Parton and Power started checking the names of companies with the registrar, through the city directory and criss-crosses, to acquire as many facts and names as they could. They worked quietly, collecting data, talking to investors, and avoiding tipping their hands to the scheme's U.S. principals before they had enough knowledge of the scheme to know what they were talking about. They worked the phones, but – and this is important – they also used their legs. They visited the registered address for one of the companies involved, and discovered that the premises were vacant. The company had never moved in. But in the lane behind the offices, Parton and Power found a dumpster. They did what any good reporter should do. They looked inside.

Now, poking around someone's garbage might seem a touch unsterile, and maybe even downright trashy and rude, but it can also be effective. Inside the garbage bin they found documents connecting the Canadian scheme to the already-failed U.S. operation. Some states had frozen bank accounts and shut down the scheme. Worried U.S. investors were fighting those actions in court but, according to documents found in the trash, they were also secretly investing in Canada, hoping to recover their investments from unsuspecting Canadians.

It was, says Parton, a lucky break. Doubly so, because they identified the dumpster before the garbage was collected. Armed with their new-found data, the team contacted the U.S. princi-pals by phone. They used a "golly gee" attitude in an attempt to gather as much incriminating evidence as possible without alerting the scam artists that they already had some dirt on the scheme. And the principals talked, making wild statements: the Canadian in charge of the scheme was also "head of the Canadian lottery"; the scheme must be okay because "it had been passed by Parliament"; the milk culture "eats cancer cells."

It is an old adage of interviewers that if you give people a chance to open their mouths, sometimes they'll say the darndest things. The things they said had to be checked out by Parton and Power – it's embarrassing to phone the head of the B.C. Cancer Control Agency and ask him if yogurt eats cancer cells – but each bizarre statement gave the reporters ammunition for their story, and gave readers the chance to understand that they might not make money by investing in the scheme.

By the time Parton and Power were able to complete their investigation, they figure that British Columbians had invested between $1 million and $2 million in milk cultures. That meant that those people had lost their money forever, but the story alerted others to the scheme and helped them avoid losing their money. The findings of the reporters also alerted Canadian regulatory agencies to the scam, and several of the people involved were charged with criminal acts.

And speaking of criminal acts, the legalities of diving into someone else's garbage are questionable. Anyone using the technique could meet the fate of Global TV's Doug Small, the Ottawa reporter who was given leaked details of the federal budget a day before the government released the document. Small was charged with the criminal offence of being in possession of stolen documents. If you have any questions about the legality of a research technique, check with your lawyer before making it public.

ENVIRONMENT

WITH A FEW WEEKS TO GO before voting day in the 1988 federal election, the abortion issue seemed hot in B.C.'s Okanagan area. Conservatives, Liberals, and New Democrats were juggling their personal stands on the no-win issue with the wishes of the electorate, with most of them wishing not to talk about it. But the campaign manager for one of the Conservative candidates, a staunch anti-abortionist, calmly folded his arms and told me abortion was not an issue to worry about in this campaign. The claim was hard to believe – residents in Kamloops and Vernon had battled for years to control their local hospital boards, with anti-abortionists fighting pro-choice neighbours to vote for people who either would or would not allow abortions to be performed at local hospitals.

"I don't know why you're asking about abortion," the campaign manager said. "Abortion was yesterday's issue." He took me aside and told me that pollsters for his party had conducted surveys of thousands of Canadian voters to determine the issue uppermost in their minds. According to public opinion polls and attitudinal surveys, it wasn't abortion or unemployment or inflation or separation, the traditional bugbears of Canadian politics. It wasn't even free trade, although the debates between the three federal leaders had turned on that controversial subject.

Instead, the number one priority of most Canadians was a topic long considered to be the darling of the left wing in this country – the environment. Conservative candidates had been coached by their handlers to talk about fresh air and water, about how they would clean up the land and the seas and save the planet. That's what Canadians wanted to talk about, the campaign manager said. I didn't believe him. I was wrong.

Twenty years ago, politicians in this province had won re-election by explaining that the noxious air pollution from pulp mills was "the smell of money." Twenty years ago it was radical chic and an act of rebellion to wear the logo of Greenpeace on a jean jacket sleeve. Now B.C.'s giant corporate polluters are naming environmentalists to their boards, realizing they are going to have to be seen, at least, as trying to stop poisoning the planet. Even the bluest of Conservatives want to be known as conservationists.

This province spawned Greenpeace, and Greenpeace begat the Sea Shepherd Society, and long-haired hippie freaks set out in rickety boats to stop the testing of nuclear bombs and to save the whales. A generation later, the Vancouver offices of Greenpeace were just one part of an international network of environmentalists. In B.C., groups had been formed to save local marshes and protect the ozone layer, to preserve forested valleys and recycle plastic. The baby boomers were abandoning a lifestyle centering on conspicuous consumption for a small-is-beautiful mission of saving what we had.

Reporters seeking information or comments on environmental issues once had two choices: phone Greenpeace or SPEC. In the summer of 1989, Vancouver *Sun* environmental reporter Glenn Bohn printed out the computer list of contacts he had developed to cover his beat. Single-spaced, it came out to 12½ feet long. It has grown since then. From the Alberni Environmental Coalition to the Yalakom Ecological Society in Lillooet, hundreds of groups had been formed to protect the parts of the earth that interested them most. Thousands of people are giving up their free time to chain themselves to backhoes or write letters to government.

For the growing army of reporters covering the environment beat, it is hard to keep track of the people who call themselves environmentalists. Even big business has got into the act, creating their own special interest groups and spokesmen to compete for media time with more grassroots groups. Every group has its own special interest, and its own definition of just what it means to be an environmentalist. One group defines environmentalism as clear-cut logging to strip a mountainside bare of any visible vegetation, while others say environmentalism means not daring to touch a tree, allowing all stands of timber to rot in the forest and fall without making a sound. As with any self-proclaimed expert (see UNIVERSITIES), researchers must take care in determining the truth, and must never rely on the statements of just one group. For this book, reporter Bohn analyzed his contact list for the names of organizations that researchers might start with. Other organizations were catalogued by a team of Vancouver *Province* reporters and editors in an extensive series on the environment which ran in that paper in the fall of 1989. The following list is by no means a full rundown of every environmental group in the province. It is an introduction for people looking for information about how they can do their part to protect the environment, or looking for pointers on what to do – and what pitfalls to avoid – while setting up their own environmental groups.

As for all the phone numbers: time passes and numbers change. These were current at the time of writing.

The B.C. Environmental Network helps to put people in touch with groups interested in environmental, peace, and Native Indian issues. In Vancouver, (604) 733-2400. Outside the Lower Mainland, 1-800-663-7827.

The B.C. Conservation Foundation works to preserve and enhance wildlife and habitat. (604) 533-2616.

The B.C. Wildlife Federation is the largest conservation group in B.C., with 38,000 members representing 160 clubs. (604) 576-8288.

Ducks Unlimited develops and preserves wetland habitat. (604) 591-1104.

The Federation of Mountain Clubs of B.C. represents a panorama of organizations interested in patterns and changes in policies affecting mountain users. (604) 737-3053.

The Greenpeace Foundation has more than 70,000 members in Canada and two million worldwide, and now concentrates primarily on marine and nuclear issues and pollution control. (604) 736-0321.

The Outdoor Recreation Council of B.C. represents 47 umbrella organizations with a total membership of 100,000. (604) 737-3058.

The Recycling Council of B.C. is an association of companies, groups, societies, and government involved in recycling and waste management. (604) 731-7222.

The Sierra Club is almost a century old, with a worldwide membership of 400,000. The Sierra Club of Western Canada has 1,500 members and is headquartered in Victoria. (604) 386-5255.

The Society Promoting Environmental Concern (SPEC) is a 500-member organization formed in 1969. (604) 736-7732.

The Western Canada Wilderness Committee has 3,100 members concerned with preserving wilderness areas and promoting responsible forest management. (604) 731-6716 or (604) 731-9799.

The West Coast Environmental Law Association offers legal advocacy on environmental issues. (604) 684-7378.

FINANCIAL
DISCLOSURE ACT

FOR TWO YEARS IT SAT in a filing cabinet under the feet of reporters in the Victoria parliamentary press gallery – a document which would bring down a pair of cabinet ministers. For two years, reporters had quick and easy access to the document which would lead them to learn that provincial cabinet ministers owned chunks of a timber company partnership which could benefit from decisions those ministers made. For two years, the document was updated regularly, spelling out in bold black ink on white paper that the Honourable Tom Waterland, minister of Forests, had invested his own money in a consortium which stood to benefit from logging of the South Moresby area of the Queen Charlotte Islands, a region long the subject of a bitter Haida land clam. Waterland wasn't the only politician owning a piece of the company. Energy Minister Stephen Rogers also owned a share. Rogers could make or break forestry companies by setting the price they paid for hydro-electric power.

Finally, CBC radio reporter Barry Bell stumbled onto the document and exposed the conflicts of interest which eventually led to Waterland's resignation and charges against Rogers.

The documents were public disclosure forms, filed by every MLA and municipal official (including members of park boards, councils, and school boards) in B.C. Under the province's Financial Disclosure Act, passed by the NDP government in 1974, politicians must disclose their holdings of shares or companies in forms updated between January 1 and 15 and July 1 and 15. The law is designed to avoid conflicts of interest. The disclosures are not policed or checked in any way until the media bring up problems.

Municipal officials file their documents at the municipal hall. MLAs file them with the Clerk of the House. They are not accessible by phone – researchers must peruse them personally – but they are available for the asking. The trouble in Victoria was that no reporters with the press gallery were asking. The reason? A combination of overwork and inexperience. Reporters who knew about the Financial Disclosure Act checked the forms when they could, but they were battling deadlines and pressure from editors to produce soft and fluffy stories, or to "match" whatever stories the competing news agencies were carrying. Former Vancouver *Sun* legislative reporter Lisa Fitterman said that she had never examined the disclosures "because nobody told me the bloody things existed."

Waterland and Rogers regularly updated their forms, revealing in all honesty what they owned. But no one read them.

Bell eventually won a well-deserved award from the Centre for Investigative Journalism for his exposure of the scandals, but the press gallery was embarrassed by the fact that the ammunition they needed to bring down a pair of cabinet ministers sat for two years in an office they had to walk past each day to get to work. The highly respected columnist Marjorie Nichols said the problem was caused by a lack of direction from editors, and a newsroom propensity for parachuting junior reporters into press galleries.

"It's the lack of continuity," she said at the time. "You can't just inject things into people's brains, and teach them about the history of the B.C. legislature. But don't blame the people there. They are doing what their bosses tell them to do. We have no one to blame but ourselves."

So, for those of us who already know about the Financial Disclosure Act, it's time we ensure the disclosure forms are carefully monitored each time they are updated. For those of you who didn't know about the act...now you know. Take a look at the forms, look for something to find. Even if no scandal jumps off the page, it might be worthwhile for those of you working at community newspapers to publish a list of the holdings of your elected officials. You never know which of your readers might realize that something is amiss.

FIRE COMMISSIONER

IT'S HARD TO PUT A PRICE tag on a life. But ten bucks doesn't seem like too much to pay to save one. It would have saved the lives of two kids in Penticton, but the money wasn't spent, and now the kids are dead. The kids were tenants of a motel in Penticton, living there with their 24-year-old mother. The boy was three, his sister was one. No one knows what happened for sure, but investigators with the Penticton Fire Department suspect the boy was playing with matches. All anyone knows is that the children's mother suddenly smelled smoke, and by the time she made it to the back room where her kids were trapped, a wall of fire stood in her way. The mother suffered burns and shock. The children were killed.

If there had been warning, even a few seconds, there might have been time to save the children. A simple $10 smoke detector could have offered warning, but interviews with the motel operators determined that they hadn't installed smoke detectors. The devices are mandatory for most public buildings, but the law does not require them for structures with the kind of easy exit the single-level motel units had.

A camera crew with the CBC affiliate in Penticton had video-taped the aftermath of the motel fire, and the CBC news show in Vancouver carried the report. The deaths seemed stupid, unnecessary in an era when you can pick up a smoke detector at any drug store or supermarket. A check with the B.C. Fire Commissioner found that the number of fire deaths had plummeted during the past few years – the result of a combination of easily available smoke detectors and efficient policing of fire prevention laws. But still, each year, people were dying from fires in houses which either had no smoke detectors, or had detectors that were located in the wrong place or that were out of power.

The saddest statistic held by the Fire Commissioner's office recorded a house fire in the town of Stewart. The home had a smoke detector, but the battery was removed one night to operate a child's toy. Early the next morning, one of the boys heard his 13-year-old sister yelling "Fire!" He came out of his bedroom, kicked at his mother's door, then dove through an upstairs window. He and two of his brothers, along with their mother, escaped. Their sister and a 10-year-old mentally handicapped brother died in the flames. The boy was known to play with lighters. Cause of the fire was never determined, but investigators believe all members of the family would have escaped if the smoke detector had been operating.

Fire commission analyst Param-jit Seran records as many statistics and details as he can think of, knowing the information he divines might one day save a life. Unlike some bureaucrats, Seran is free with the information he gathers. He used his computer to analyze fires that cameramen for CBC TV News had videotaped, and determined that many of them – including several with graphic pictures of covered bodies being removed from still-smoking homes – involved homes without smoke detectors. The two-part documentary we ran on fire prevention won a commendation from the B.C. Fire Chief's Association, which noted the information might have helped to spur some people into installing fire prevention and warning devices.

That Christmas I gave smoke alarms to my friends.

Several years earlier, Seran helped to put out a fire of a different kind – the fire of fear. A Vancouver synagogue had been torched by an arsonist. No one knew the reason behind the crime, but the fear of an anti-Semitic uprising burned through many minds. At my request, Seran punched out a list of arson fires he had recorded for churches and buildings related to religion. His statistics showed that the synagogue fire was just one of several dozen church fires which had been set throughout B.C. during the previous couple of years. The list of targets sounded like a roll call of the World Council of Churches – every faith had been hit.

It seemed that churches were a favoured target for B.C. arsonists, and while the criminals may have been vandals spying an easy unguarded victim, or sociopathic loons, they appeared to be non-sectarian. While there was still fear stemming from the synagogue fire, the crime was put into perspective.

Fire chiefs in your local fire department can offer some information about fires, but the B.C. Fire Commission is the place to go when you need more.

Contact:

> The Fire Commissioner
> Suite 1 – 2780 East Broadway
> Vancouver, B.C.
> V5M 1Y8
> (604) 660-9000

For information about insurance losses due to fire, contact:

> The Insurance Bureau of Canada
> (604) 684-3635

For information about insurance crime, contact:

> The Insurance Crime Prevention Bureaux
> (604) 294-9661

GOVERNMENT AGENT

INVESTIGATORS AND RESEARCHERS working outside Vancouver or Victoria, or trying to conduct their research as inexpensively as possible, have access to a government service that saves time and money. And anyone buying a used car should use the service as well.

The resource is called Government Agents, and it's located in 60 communities throughout B.C., from Ashcroft to Williams Lake. Government Agents have access to a pair of important databases: the REGISTRAR OF COMPANIES and records of liens.

For a fee of $6, the Government Agent in your community will pull a computer printout from the B.C. government's computer which will tell you the most important details available on ownership and control of a company. The information is available by mail – with a certified cheque or a money order – and the service can also be performed in person.

Government agents also keep tabs on liens. These are charges filed against automobile owners, usually by banks which have granted loans using the car as collateral, or by mechanics who claim they haven't been paid for work performed on the vehicle. If you buy a car with a lien filed against it – even if you didn't know about the lien – you have inherited the charge and are liable for the bill or the outstanding loan. Information on liens is available by mail, although as most people are in a hurry to find out about a car they're interested in, it's best to visit your Government Agent in person. You must give the agent the full serial number of the car and its year and model. For an $8 fee, you can save yourself a lot of headaches later.

At the time of writing, this information was also available from the computer system known as BC OnLine (see COMPUTER DATABASES) for a $5 fee for each search.

INVESTIGATIVE
REPORTERS AND
EDITORS INC.

"IF YOU WANT TO understand how something works, first find out how it is supposed to work. What are the statutes, and what are the implementing regulations? What paperwork is required to document compliance? If professionals are involved, what standards do they use to evaluate themselves? And finally, what are the differences, if any, between what people say they are doing, what they are required to do (or are prohibited from doing), and what they are, in fact, doing?"

Good advice to anyone researching anything. It comes from a U.S. publication, *The Reporters' Handbook*, produced by an association called Investigative Reporters and Editors Inc. (IRE), a group of interested journalists and academics similar to Canada's CAJ (see **CANADIAN ASSOCIATION OF JOURNALISTS**), that is based at the University of Missouri. In 1983, IRE compiled a how-to guide that led through the maze of public documents and sources of material available in the United States. It was updated in 1989.

In 500 pages, the handbook offers a crisp, succinct tour of the U.S. paper trail, beginning with readily available public documents like annual budgets, and moving deeply into the arcane bureaucracy – federal and state – that only a nation of 250 million with a 200-year-old "free press" designation in its constitution could dream up. The book is written for U.S. investigators active in that country, but a well-thumbed copy should sit on the bookshelf (alongside Overbury's *Finding Canadian Facts Fast*) of any Canadian researcher as well. Canada's branch plant economy is heavily dependent on the actions of U.S. firms and U.S. people, and investigations into anything Canadian often lead researchers to U.S. sources. Now, with the Free Trade Agreement, those connections will tighten.

To those of us in B.C., the U.S. bureaucracy is foreign and unknown. (The same holds true for the Canadian bureaucratic process.) But the authors and editors of the IRE handbook help any B.C. researchers get a handle on manoeuvering through U.S. documentation to find what they're looking for. The book is broken into simple chapters, and includes sections on mastering the U.S. Freedom of Information Act, tracking down U.S. government publications, backgrounding people, tracing land sales, investigating health care, cops, courts, labour, schools and businesses (see TEN-K).

The book seems daunting at first, fat and full of facts, but it's laid out in easily digestible chunks, allowing researchers to flip through pages to find what they're looking for. A word of advice: when you get it, give it a quick read front to back. You won't memorize the tens of thousands of key documents and sources, but the information will sit at the back of your brain, and when you come across something in your daily routine, a warning bell will go off, reminding you that you once came across a U.S. source for the information. Then go back to the book and look up the specific reference to the public document you need.

For journalists using the book, U.S. newsman Patrick Riordan notes that "records are no substitute for shoeleather or sources. To make your story come alive, you ultimately have to talk to real people on the record. But knowing how to run the records comprehensively can help you ask better questions."

The Reporters' Handbook also recounts scores of investigations by some of the top reporters in the U.S. If you read how they did it, you get a good idea how you can do it too.

The book can be ordered through bookstores – it's published by

St. Martin's Press of New York – or by writing directly to the publisher's Vancouver representative:

Nelson Canada
201-2125 York Avenue
Vancouver, B.C.
V6K 1C4

LAND TITLES OFFICE

YOU WERE INTRODUCED to Donald Gutstein in **ASSESSMENT AUTHORITY OF B.C.** While Gutstein notes that the Assessment Authority is a good place to begin searching for information about land holdings, he calls the B.C. Land Titles Office "the key source" for information about society's most expensive, and usually most controversial, resource: land.

Anyone who owns a piece of land in this province must register it with the Land Titles Office serving the area of B.C. in which that person lives. Registering the land ensures that someone cannot fraudulently lay claim to owning the property. Registering land also leaves a paper trail that can be followed to determine who bought what, at what price, and who sold it.

The Vancouver People's Law School has published a handy pamphlet, *Land Transactions*, which summarizes the legal processes used in buying and selling land. It notes that the government-supervised Land Titles Office retains the originals of all documents – including deeds, mortgages, and agreements for sale – protecting them against loss, fire, or theft. The documents are also microfilmed, and the microfilm is available to the public.

Names can be changed and companies can be formed to camouflage the identity of investors, but when the subject is land, the records of the Land Titles Office are available to the public and are surprisingly revealing. There are LTOs serving each of the province's eight judicial districts. (Addresses can be found in the blue pages of the phone book under Government of B.C. listings: Land Titles).

Don't be surprised by the hubbub and frenetic activity the first time you enter an LTO. The people scurrying from filing cabinet to microfiche screen are usually digging up information for real estate agents and lawyers. The land market is big business, and they have got to be quick to make sure they're buying, selling, or registering the correct piece of land.

We can be more laid back. Although the system may appear daunting, clerks at the LTO will offer any assistance you need to find what you're looking for. What you need to start is the legal description of the land. Street addresses aren't used in the world of the LTO. Instead, pieces of property are registered under a system identifying them as part of a municipal planning map.

For example, the street address of Bill Vander Zalm's Fantasy Garden World is 10800 Number 5 Road, Richmond. The land falls into the area administered by the New Westminster Land Titles Office. The legal description – available from the local city hall or B.C. Assessment Authority office – is "Lot 56, Section 31, Block 4 North, Range 5 West, Plan 36037."

Take heart. You don't have to know what all that means. All you have to know is the legal description. Armed with that, the clerks at the LTO will find you the background you need. The information stored at the LTO can tell you the owner of a piece of land and the date of its registration, the previous owners, mortgages and mortgage holders, and other charges against the property, such as builder's liens and agreements for sale.

Among the key documents are:

Certificate of Indefeasible Title ($2 search fee)

This document includes the identity of the property's owner and certificate number, the previous certificate number, the date the transfer was registered, and a list of all charges – mortgages, liens, etc. – against the property.

Transfer of Estate in Fee-Simple (on microfiche. 50 cents for each page photocopied.)

This used to be called the "deed." Now, in the LTO bureaucracy, it's a "Form 23." It gives the name of the previous owner, the new owner, the market value, the selling price (sometimes), and the lawyer who handled the transaction.

Mortgage

Yes, the mortgage. This document tells you the identity of the individual or financial institution holding the mortgage, the amount of the mortgage, and the interest rate and monthly payment. If the mortgage has been paid off, a document called the Discharge of Mortgage will be registered in the LTO.

Builder's Lien

A "charge" against the property filed by a contractor, subcontractor, material supplier, or workers involved in construction or renovations. The lien claims that work has been performed on the property which has not been paid for. The property can be sold to pay for the work. And anyone purchasing the land before the lien has been discharged winds up acquiring the lien and inheriting the debt or charge.

Right to Purchase

This document – another "charge" – is an agreement for sale between the owner of the land and a person wishing to buy it, in which the seller finances the sale. This document tells you that the seller retains ownership of the property until the entire loan has been paid off.

Option to Purchase and Right of First Refusal

Both documents are records of agreements between a buyer and a seller of a piece of land. Under the Option to Purchase, the holder of the option has paid money to the owner of a piece of land for the right to buy the property within a certain time period, usually at a stated price. The People's Law School notes that the option does not obligate the holder of the option to purchase the land.

The Right of First Refusal is an agreement that if the owner of a piece of land decides to sell the property, the owner must offer it to the holder of the Right of First Refusal. It does not mean the land-owner must sell the property – just that the holder of the right of first refusal has the first chance to buy the property or match any other offers.

The Right of First Refusal is often used by people or companies wishing to buy up large blocks of land, or get property rezoned. If the property you're looking at has a Right of First Refusal charged to it, there's a good chance it's a prime candidate for development.

So, with the legal description of Fantasy Gardens, researchers like Gutstein visit the Land Titles Office and discover that Vander Zalm in 1986 acquired a mortgage for $2 million on his theme park from the Canadian Imperial Bank of Commerce, paying interest of one percent above the minimum lending rate set by the bank.

LTO documents can also reveal which members of a municipal council or their friends stand to profit from a local rezoning, which school board members have flipped property prior to an important decision to build a new high school, etc. It's simple, it's accessible to any member of the public, and it's almost free.

If you can't visit an LTO on your own because you live too far away or are battling a deadline, private companies which advertise in the Yellow Pages under the listing Title Services will conduct a search for you at a fee of about $50 per search. As well, the computer system called BC OnLine (see COMPUTER DATABASES) contains information about registered owners of land and historical title, but does not include details about encumbrances.

LANDLORDS

SHARON BACKUS WAS 15 when she died, falling from a fourth-floor balcony of an apartment in Vancouver's West End. The city police had caught her turning a trick on a mattress on the floor with a 33-year-old city man. Backus told police she was getting some identification, slipped onto the balcony, and tried to climb to freedom. It was a ploy the young runaway from Winnipeg had used successfully before, but this time she didn't make it. She clung to the metal railing of the balcony for as long as she could, then, without a word, slipped with a thud onto the concrete below. She lay in a coma for six days before dying.

Just another dead hooker. Another street kid that no one much cares about, another commodity used by men who have the price it takes to buy a child for sex. The death of Sharon Backus didn't even make it into the newspapers at first. It was no big deal. Not a murder, not a prominent person. Just one of the 200 or so youngsters who worked the streets of the West End in the early 1980s, turning tricks to buy the drugs they needed to banish the shame of the tricks they turned to buy the drugs.

The police issued no press release the day that Sharon Backus fell to her death. No crime had been commited, and the cops didn't consider the event "news" – something worth bringing up at the news conference police hold each weekday morning at 9:15 at police headquarters. As a reporter for the Vancouver *Sun* who had written a number of stories on child prostitution, I seemed as likely as anyone else for a friend of a friend of Sharon Backus' mother to call with a tip that the death should warrant a news story.

Contacted in Winnipeg, Sharon's mother repeated the litany that's been heard too often before – Sharon was a "normal" kid from a single-parent welfare home, had started experimenting with drugs and hanging out with street people at the age of 12, had dabbled in petty theft and minor crime, lured to freewheeling Vancouver at the age of 14 to turn tricks and do drugs.

"Are you going to write a story?" she asked. "You should write a story about the adults. About how nothing happens to the adults."

Indeed, the "adults" were part of the story of child prostitution that hadn't been fully explored. It was easy for reporters like myself to write stories about the tragically short life and times of the victims of child prostitution, but we had never been able to crack the flip side of the story – the men who used these children for sex. The reason for that was simple: it was easy to find kids working on street corners, but it was harder to interview the men who drove silently through the city streets, picking up the children for a few minutes of sex for dollars, usually performed in their cars. The men were the victimizers – along with the society that allowed the practice of child prostitution to continue – but the men were harder to find. They had money, for the most part, and jobs, the kind of respectability that dollars can buy.

Sharon's mother felt her daughter's death deserved a story, but facts were not readily available. All the mother knew was that Sharon had left Winnipeg with an 18-year-old male prostitute named Eric Goodman. All I knew was the address of the apartment that Sharon Backus fell from. And the apartment manager wasn't much help. All he knew was that Goodman had vanished without leaving a forwarding address, that the only furniture was a bare mattress on the floor, that other tenants had reported that

Sharon and Eric usually appeared stoned, and that one of the tenants had once accused Sharon of stealing towels from the laundry room.

But the landlord checked his files for me. Most landlords demand extensive credit information from anyone renting a home. That information is neither confidential nor public. There is no requirement that landlords release tenancy information to inquirers, but there is also no restriction against releasing it. Some landlords will refuse to cooperate. Others, like this man, will listen to the researcher's reasons and decide to help out. According to the files, the apartment was not listed in the name of Goodman or of Backus. The renter of record was a 40-year-old man named David Andersen, who gave a permanent address in the Vancouver suburb of North Delta. According to the information filed in the landlord's forms, Andersen earned $20,000 a year from his job as manager of the lingerie department of Woodward's department store at the Lansdowne Shopping Mall in Richmond, had recently paid off a 1976 Ford Granada, and was married with several children. The files revealed his Social Insurance Number, his driver's license number, and even the number of his account with the Bank of Montreal.

The only thing the landlord's file didn't answer was this: why was a suburban family man paying $350 a month for a "trick pad" being used by a 19-year-old male hooker and a 15-year-old female hooker?

Andersen didn't want to talk to me. I asked him what a 15-year-old girl was doing living in an apartment in his name, with only a mattress on the floor for furniture. His response: "I never gave it any thought." He said he had met Goodman – then 17 – at a bar in Winnipeg, and had rented the apartment for him. "I've done nothing wrong," he said. "Why are you talking to me? I'm not responsible for her death. I'm not responsible for all the world's misfortunes. I didn't push her."

Indeed, he hadn't. No one had. Not really. Vancouver society had decided it was okay for 15-year-old runaways to turn tricks in naked apartments in the city's West End, and if the apartment happened to be paid for by a respected white-collar family man, that was okay too. The Vancouver *Sun* was pleased with my report on the life and death of Sharon Backus, but former managing editor Bruce Larsen wanted just one thing changed. Remove the reference to Andersen and his place of employment, he said. I refused. The story ran without my byline, and without the reference to Woodward's.

Mac Parry, the editor of *Vancouver* Magazine, commissioned a longer, more detailed account of the story for his publication. Parry said he was satisfied with my story, but former publisher Ron Stern, a Vancouver lawyer, took a look at the piece and said he too wanted the reference to Woodward's removed.

Why? I asked.

Stern flipped over the latest copy of his magazine. Woodward's had bought an ad on the back page, the most expensive page of all. "We live in the real world," he said.

A few months after the *Sun* stories ran, Vancouver Coroner Larry Campbell conducted an inquest into the death. He said Sharon Backus was responsible for some of her actions, "but I would suggest that the greater portion must be borne by the persons surrounding her. In this tragic and sometimes revolting case, it would take a complete turnaround by a certain segment of our society to ensure that a person like Sharon did not turn to prostitution as a way of inserting some excitement and self-esteem into her life. Sharon is a victim of the segment of the adult population that takes advantage of weakness and unhappiness in others. No recommendations will ever do away with this despicable group of humanity."

Andersen testified for a couple of hours at the inquest then went back to his job.

If you're looking for a street person who has no known address, you might try a method that was successful for me with another dead child hooker. A few months after the Backus story, the body of another 15-year-old was found in a ditch in Ladner. Rochelle Dawn Gray had been using heroin and cocaine, a numbing combination which would have helped to mask the pain of a pelvic inflammation which had spread through her body and into her bowels and intestines. Gray had died partially from a disease caused by the sex that adult men had bought. The discovery of her body had warranted a two-paragraph story in the *Sun*, but city editor Ian Haysom assigned me to try to find out more on the death.

No one on Davie Street knew anything about a kid called Rochelle Dawn Gray. I spent hours talking to street people, kids, cops, contacts, and got nowhere. Finally I asked Rochelle's father to give me a copy of his daughter's most recent high school photo, the one taken before she had hit the streets for good. The *Sun*'s photographers blew up the picture, and I returned downtown. It took less than an hour for a friend of Rochelle's to recognize the photo.

"That's Angel!" she screamed. Then she wept. On the street, kids don't use their real names. They adopt street names, and friendships are formed between children who know each other by no other name. On the street they called her Angel, and on the street, her friends told me what they knew.

MINUTES

VANCOUVER SUN REPORTER Jeff Lee sat in a Penticton laundromat, fiddling with a pay phone, trying to get a clear phone line so he could hook up his lap-top computer to file a story to his newsroom. A frustrating experience, but sweetened the next day when Premier Bill Vander Zalm announced that, as a result of Lee's story, Tourism Minister Bill Reid had resigned amid revelations that he had improperly directed government funds to friends.

As the *Sun*'s regional affairs reporter, Lee's beat included the city councils of the dozen Vancouver suburbs. The information needed to break the story that would cause Reid to step down was available on public documents and committee minutes, but it was an impossible task to expect one reporter to read the bales of paper generated daily by each city hall. Lee got a phone call from a contact advising him that members of White Rock city council were concerned about a grant that a local charity had received to develop a recycling system for that community's garbage. The tipster said the money had wound up being paid to a company controlled by a political associate of Reid.

A hot lead, but it had to be proven. The charity was called the Semiahmoo House Society, an organization that found work for mentally handicapped people. A phone call to Semiahmoo

House determined that the charity had received a grant of $277,000 from a provincial agency called GO B.C. to operate a curbside recycling program. Semiahmoo House had found the whole situation rather peculiar – the charity hadn't even asked for a grant. The money just showed up.

In fact, half of the money had already been spent, the official said. It had gone to a local company called Eco Clean, which was developing a system involving a fleet of trucks and three separate plastic boxes which would hold recyclable glass, paper, and metal. Lee conducted a company search (see **REGISTRAR OF COMPANIES**) which revealed that Eco Clean was controlled by two men: George Doonan and Bill Sullivan.

Lee confirmed the connection to Reid by scouring his newsroom for old campaign literature from the 1984 provincial election. A brochure touting Reid as the Socred to vote for listed his campaign manager: George Doonan. So far, so good. But there was still no clear connection that Reid had ensured the money went to his crony. Lee went hunting. White Rock city hall told him the recycling program was developed as part of a joint White Rock-Surrey beautification program administered by a collection of community boosters from both municipalities known as the Community Pride Committee. The committee did its job well. It kept minutes of all meetings, detailed notes outlining who said what. White Rock city hall had copies of the minutes which quoted Reid saying that he wanted every B.C. community to purchase the products of Eco Clean. In fact, the minister had said that municipalities which had already invested in recycling products from other companies would be reimbursed by the B.C. government if they switched to Eco Clean.

Semiahmoo House confirmed that Reid had told the charity to sign a contract with Eco Clean.

Lee had his story. Sullivan confirmed in a phone call that he was a long-time family friend of Bill Reid. Lee had researched the story during the weekend. On Monday, he flew to Penticton to cover an already-assigned annual meeting of the Union of B.C. Municipalities, so he had to work the phones to unearth the rest of the facts from his Penticton hotel room. By Tuesday night he had put together the details, and filed his story through his computer modem.

As it turned out, Vander Zalm was in Penticton to address the UBCM meeting, and the premier called a special news conference shortly after Lee's story hit the streets in Vancouver. Lee expected to hear that the premier was investigating the affair. Instead, "I was astounded," he recalls. Vander Zalm told the assembled reporters that Reid had resigned. The minister was currently in Hungary on government business, but was returning home immediately. Bill Reid had been one of Vander Zalm's allies when the premier first announced his intention to seek the leadership of the Social Credit party, but Vander Zalm acted swiftly when the story broke.

Lee notes that the information he needed for the story was all available in public documents. "Don't ever underestimate the value of minutes," he says. Memories can become fuzzy and fade, "but documents stay fresh."

B.C.'s Auditor General launched an investigation into Lee's findings, and determined that Reid had acted improperly. At the time of this writing, most of the $277,000 is still sitting in trust accounts, while the B.C. government decides if it will attempt to recover the cash.

OFF THE RECORD

"INFORMATION WHICH THE PUBLIC should know about is sometimes only available through a confidential source. 'Off-the-record' discussions with journalists, for example, are often held with public figures and others. If the confidentiality of sources were not respected as a matter of principle, this would inhibit the free flow of information which is essential to the vitality of a democratic society."

The above paragraph is a quote from the Canadian Broadcasting Corporation's Journalistic Policy handbook, a guide to what CBC journalists can and cannot do. But if it's followed to the letter, it could drastically hurt reporters and their sources. That is because the CBC fails to distinguish between the concept of confidentiality, and the concept of off the record.

The section discussing communication on **BACKGROUND** stressed that some information can be sensitive enough to get a source into serious trouble if the source of the information is identified. Usually, sources will agree to talk on background, which means their identities are kept secret even though the facts are made public. But sometimes the information is just too sensitive. The source knows that the leak would be traced. If that happens, the source could lose a job, or worse.

In that case, conversations are usually held off the record. The

CBC's explanation implies that off-the-record information from the mythical "public figures" can be used as long as the identities of the sources are kept secret. But that is only the case with background briefings.

If something is off the record, it is off the record – it didn't happen. The reporter cannot use the information in a story attributed to an unnamed source. In fact, the reporter has guaranteed that the information and the source will be kept secret. That commitment usually means the reporter must devise a way to obtain the information again – often by acquiring the official documents which will confirm the off-the-record information.

That entails more research, more digging. It's time-consuming and frustrating to chase after information that you already have, but that's the commitment you make to someone when you speak off the record.

The simplest solution: ensure the source knows the difference between "off the record" and "background." Talk to the source. Explain how the information would be used, and how the confidentiality of the source will be maintained. Usually a source will agree to talk for background, as long as the identity of the source is protected. An important warning: always make sure that both sides understand the rules of the game before the conversation begins. Too often reporters wind up obtaining wonderful information from a source who, at the end of the conversation, adds, "Oh. And that's off the record."

When that happens, the general rule of thumb kicks in: it's too late. The conversation was held on the record and for the record. It happened and it's fair game. If the source wants to remain confidential, the source must get that commitment from the reporter before the sensitive stuff is discussed.

Allan Fotheringham used to say that he had a simple response when he heard the words "off the record" – he ran away. As fast as he could. Because he knew that by making the guarantee of keeping something a secret, he could play into the hands of a tricky politician who knows the best way to keep something a secret is to get the other players to promise to keep it a secret too.

PHOTOCOPY

THIS IS A VERY SHORT chapter. But it is essential to anyone doing research. It will not tell you how to find information. But it will tell you how to keep information. The message can be contained in three words: make a photocopy.

Of everything you get. Particularly of sensitive material. Use the photocopy as the document you work with, and work from. Keep the original document in a safe place, a place where it cannot be lost, a place where you can lay your hands on it quickly. Why do I say this? Because there is a black hole in every office, be it newsroom or basement study. It is the hole into which odd socks and disposable pens and cigarette lighters fall, the hole that sucks things in and never gives them up. (There is a school of thought that says the socks, lighters, and pens are processed inside the black hole and are returned to the world as wire hangers in dark closets, but that's a theory I don't believe.) Bits of paper also fall into this hole. They become lost and gone forever.

The documents you acquire if you use this book – land titles, Revenue Canada reports, insider trading reports, et al. – form the spine of your stories or findings. While they're not hard to get, the process of acquiring them can be time-consuming. Every researcher has, at some time, discovered that important documents – whether they're "smoking guns" or just essential background material – have fallen into the black hole. Tears don't help. Punching holes into walls doesn't help. Kicking the cat doesn't help. Bits of paper vanish on their own and, like diplomats in Beirut, nothing can get them back.

But if you keep a backup file, containing copies or originals of all the crucial documentation, you can defeat the black hole and complete your project. The photocopier machine is a Godsend to researchers. With a coin and the push of a button, essential documents can be copied and tucked away into a file folder, to be forgotten about until they're needed. Do the same thing with notebooks. Notes get lost too, but if you photocopy them and tuck them away, you can avoid hours of frustration, or hours of re-doing the interview.

The backup file is also important for an entirely different reason: graphics. Sensitive documents – secret memos, confidential government reports – can sometimes be photographed for inclusion in a newspaper or magazine story. Television news and documentary productions have to "show" what they're talking about. If the broadcast narrator mentions a document, the pictures on the screen must show that document. But researchers are notorious for dribbling coffee on their documents, or for doodling, underlining, and otherwise defacing sensitive and important material. If you photocopy the original and then work from the photocopy, the original document will go unscathed, ready to be photographed for the final report or submitted as evidence when such evidence is required.

Along these same lines, never, ever, ever trust a computer. This might sound like an admonition from a Luddite who learned to write on an Underwood instead of an IBM and, in fact, it is. But I've found the most user-friendly computers will turn rogue, swallowing stories and reports, collaborating with the black hole to ruin your life. I once met the husband of a Ph.D candidate who noted that he had a computer disk in his pocket which held his wife's doctoral dissertation. The information on the disk represented two years of work. Neither the student nor her husband had made a backup disk. They hadn't printed the story to make a hard copy. The life-work of the student was on a disk that could be erased by an errant magnetic wave or scratchy surface. While floppy disks can save time and space, they can also be damaged, and the information they hold can be lost.

The standard rule of thumb is this: if you have information you couldn't bear to lose, make a copy. If you've written enough stuff on your computer that you'd cry if it were lost, make a printout.

Where should you store valuable documents or floppy disks? If you can afford it, rent a safe-deposit box at your local bank or credit union. For a few dollars a month, your material will be safe from fire, theft, and black holes. If you don't want to take the trouble, and you don't have a guaranteed fire-proof safe at your home or office, put your papers where your mayonnaise is: in your fridge. Storing documents inside a refrigerator won't necessarily protect them from acts of malice or of God, but the inside of a fridge is probably the safest place in any home in event of fire. Your office could burn down tomorrow, but the fridge will likely be left standing. Most floppy disk manufacturers warn that their product should not be stored at temperatures less than 10 degrees Celsius, so the fridge trick is not recommended for computer information.

PROFESSIONAL
ASSOCIATIONS

THE TINY COMMUNITY of Alert Bay was in shock. One of the town's doctors was dead by his own hand. Area residents had known the man as a friend. But they had also known the man as Doctor Robert Rifleman. As it turned out, that was not his real name, and he was not a doctor, even though he had performed surgery in the local hospital and had assisted at a pair of Caesarean section births.

The dead man was actually a U.S. citizen named Roberto Enrique Trujillo, a navy veteran who practised medicine under a host of phony identities throughout the U.S., Mexico, and finally, in Canada. Trujillo would steal identity papers from real doctors and set up practice, sometimes as a physician, other times as a psychologist. Authorities suspect that Trujillo taught himself medical techniques during the time he spent in U.S. prisons for such offences as kidnapping, robbery, and assault. Trujillo was operating a clinic for indigents in the Mexican town of San Miguel de Allende in 1978, posing as a Dr. Falcon. Dr. Robert Rifleman started working with Trujillo, but quickly became convinced that the "doctor" was a fake, and accused him of incompetence.

Trujillo stole Rifleman's papers and fled Mexico, travelled to Seattle, and then to Alert Bay, on a small island off the north coast of Vancouver Island. He set up shop in the local hospital, treating patients, making friends. But the real Dr. Rifleman had returned home and advised his local College of Physicians and Surgeons – the governing body for medical doctors – that he was resuming his U.S. practice.

The College was perplexed; according to its records, Rifleman was already practising in Alert Bay. The professional association asked Rifleman to clarify his situation, and Trujillo's house of cards came tumbling down. The RCMP were alerted, Trujillo was arrested, and in a jail cell on January 27, 1980, Roberto Enrique Trujillo performed his last piece of surgery. He smashed his eyeglasses on the cell toilet, and used a shard of glass to slit his wrist and his neck. He died instantly.

The Mounties now had a body on their hands, and an inquest would have to be held. The RCMP had the details, but wouldn't release anything to the public or to the press. However, the "Dr. Robert Rifleman" identity was all that was needed to trace his background.

The United States is a big place with a lot of doctors, and there was no way of knowing just where the true Robert Rifleman might be living. But most libraries, hospitals, and even doctors' offices contain a book called the *American Medical Dictionary*, which lists every practising physician in the U.S.A. Doctors are listed in alphabetical order. It took just a few seconds of looking under the Rs to find that Dr. Robert Rifleman was practising in a Wisconsin town called Steven's Point. Directory assistance had a phone number, and Dr. Robert Rifleman was talkative enough to help piece together the strange facts of the life and times of Roberto Enrique Trujillo, the man who would be a doctor.

Doctors in B.C. are members of the B.C. College of Physicians and Surgeons, which can tell you if a doctor is licensed to practise medicine, and where the practice is located. But doctors are not alone in being listed in directories. The Law Society of B.C. keeps track of lawyers, and can tell you where they can be found (it also publishes a directory of contacts in the legal profession that researchers can go to for information about legal matters). Phone (604) 669-2533.

In fact, every professional organization has a governing body which compiles lists of members. Whether they're professional engineers or dentists, social workers or golfers, fishermen or truck loggers, even hairdressers and roofing contractors, almost anyone who is important enough to be found has joined some type of professional organization. . . and that organization keeps a mailing list or a membership directory.

The lists are compiled so that professionals can communicate with each other, but they are also usually open to public scrutiny with nothing more than a phone call.

The Vancouver Yellow Pages list more than a hundred associations operating in that city. Most of them are the headquarters for the entire province. You'll also find a publication called *Directory of Associations in Canada* at your local public library, which will help you find the association that your target may belong to.

Remember that associations are not confined to occupations. If a person is a graduate of a college or university, there's a good chance that the school's alumni association has an address for its member. Even reporters can be unearthed: the Canadian Association of Journalists publishes a directory of its members including, for most, home addresses and phone numbers. Trade unions also keep track of their members, and will either help you find who you're looking for, or at least pass a message to the person for you.

So if you're looking for someone, ask yourself this: what kind of associations will that person belong to? Let your fingers do the walking, and ask politely. If the person exists, you will find them.

(A postscript: for more on the province's doctors, the Ministry of Health publishes an annual report called "The Medical Services Commission Financial Statements." It lists the payments the government has made to the province's doctors for that year. These are lump sum payments, not wages. They cover the doctor's overhead as well as his or her take-home pay. But the information can be worthwhile if you're looking into the circumstances of a particular medical doctor.)

PUBLIC ACCOUNTS

LOOKING FOR A CONFLICT of interest? The B.C. government publishes a list of potential conflicts every year. By statute, the finance ministry must disclose the payments the government has made to every person, society, and company during the past year. These disclosures are published in a set of books called the Public Accounts, available from government book stores (see **B.C. GOVERNMENT**) and libraries.

In tiny print, the names of thousands of civil servants, government suppliers, consultants, and freelancers are listed alongside the money they were paid for that fiscal year. The ministry often doesn't enjoy this part of its job and will usually delay publication of the Public Accounts for as long as possible, so the information is more than a year out of date by the time it's made available to the public. Even with the time delay, though, it can make an important read. If you suspect that local government boosters might be on the government payroll, take a look through Public Accounts – if they've been paid, Public Accounts has made a note of it.

Freelance journalist Hubert Beyer, a member of the Victoria Press Gallery, was called up on the carpet in the late 1980s when an enterprising reporter glancing through Public Accounts noted that Beyer's name appeared in the list of people who had received money from the office of the B.C. Ombudsman. Journalists reporting on the doings of government are not supposed to be paid by the government – it's considered a conflict of interest and they can lose their right to sit in the press gallery. Cornered, Beyer admitted that he had sold some freelance editing to the Ombudsman's office. He was chagrined and promised not to do it again. (It was Beyer's fault, not the Ombudsman's, who continues to provide last-resort service to British Columbians who feel they've been wronged by government. If you can't find what you're looking for in these pages, you might try the Ombudsman. In Vancouver, phone (604) 660-1366. In Victoria, phone (604) 387-5855. Long distance: 1-800-972-8972.)

Public Accounts has been used to expose conflicts of interest more important than Beyer's embarrassment, involving municipal politicians, lobbyists, consultants, and public relations firms.

By law, similar disclosures, including staff wages, are also made in separate publications by each of the province's Crown Corporations. They are available from larger libraries or from the respective corporations.

REGISTRAR
OF COMPANIES

NO ANECDOTE. JUST a phone number: (604) 387-5101.

Memorize it, please. It's the number of the Company Search department of the Registrar of Companies in Victoria, perhaps the single most effective source of information about companies and societies in this province, and the best place to start an investigation.

Any company registered in B.C., and any society headquartered in this province, must register with the Registrar of Companies, divulging corporate addresses and a list of directors of the company or society, including home addresses for those directors. The telephone operators at Company Search will call up computerized files for those companies or societies at the request of a researcher and, within seconds, will tell you the directors.

The service is free to journalists working for established news agencies. Other researchers might find it faster to obtain the same information from their local office of the **GOVERNMENT AGENT**. Whichever one you choose, the computer files are updated regularly, and the information will disclose any corporate connections or hidden affiliations. Of course, people who are determined to hide their connection to a company or society can mask that connection with front groups or agents, but on most occasions you'll find what you're looking for from the registrar.

For example:

A shopkeeper is shot in her jewelry store in a downtown shopping mall. It's 30 minutes to deadline. Police will not release her name. A call to the registrar reveals that the president of the company is a female. A photographer speeds to the home address contained in the files, and determines from relatives that yes, she is the victim....

Members of groups around the city deny any connection to a controversial religion (see CULTS). But checks with Company Search show that the same names keep cropping up as directors of various companies and societies. Visits to their homes elicit interviews which prove connections....

A company doing business on the waterfront burns to the ground, causing thousands of litres of poisonous toxic waste to be dumped into city sewers. The only people at the company's plant are secretaries and security guards. A phone call to Company Search unearths the names of the president, chief executive officer, vice-president, and directors. One of the names seems vaguely familiar. Company Search is phoned again – yes, he is also a director of a Vancouver environmental group....

A politician announces a grant to a local business. Checks with the Registrar of Companies show that the company's president is also a director of the politician's constituency association, creating a conflict of interest....

The list goes on. Before delving into any company or society, check it out with Company Search first. It will save you from walking down countless blind alleys, and from blundering and tipping your hand to the wrong person. The Registrar of Companies will also mail you a list of any encumbrances (debts) owed by the company or society. That information is not available by phone, but can be crucial in determining problems the company or society might be dealing with.

Records of the Registrar of Companies are also available from your local GOVERNMENT AGENT – in person for a $6 fee for each company search, or by computer through the system known as BC OnLine (see COMPUTER DATABASES). Computer searches cost $5 each, so the price could mount if you have a lot of companies to look at. On a positive note, BC OnLine operates outside of office hours – 8 a.m. to 8 p.m., Monday through Saturday – so the information is accessible even after the staff of the registrar's office have gone home for the day.

Companies or societies doing business in B.C. but headquartered in other provinces can also be investigated by contacting the registrar in that province. Overbury's *Finding Canadian Facts Fast* contains a list of the registrars for all provinces and territories.

REGULATORY BODIES

FOR EVERY HUMAN ENDEAVOUR, somewhere a bureaucrat is employed to regulate it. Someone once counted the laws of this country and determined that Canadians have more rules, regulations, and rigmarole than any other society on earth. This can be a problem for anyone trying to do anything different. It can be a boon to anyone trying to find out problems and scabs in the system.

In the quote that opened the section **INVESTIGATIVE REPORTERS AND EDITORS, INC.**, the IRE advised researchers to find out how things are supposed to work, to determine if things are working improperly. It is sound advice but, unfortunately, it is too often ignored by too many reporters, researchers, and editors eager for the "quick and dirty" story – find a few facts, crank out a "news McNugget," and move on to the next assignment.

You won't find something unless you go looking for something to find, and you won't notice that you've found something out of place unless you know the places where things are supposed to be found. Trouble is, in this increasingly regulated society, no one can memorize all the changing laws and rules governing our activities. The good thing is, you don't have to.

All you have to do is look it up when you start your research project. Provincial laws are compiled in a weighty binder called

B.C. Statutes, and can be scanned in most libraries. From the Public Toilets Act to the laws governing the burial of paupers, a lawyer somewhere, sometime, has encoded the rules in print. Read the law before you start acting on a tip that laws are being broken, and you'll be far ahead of most of your competitors.

If the laws are confusing, talk to the regulatory body in charge of administering the particular human endeavour you're examining. These offices are spread too far afield for a complete list here, but the phone directory of the B.C. government (see **B.C. GOVERNMENT**) will give you quick access to a phone number to call for some fast background. For instance, opening your phone book to the section of the Ministry of Labour and Consumer Services, you'll find regulators for such diverse activities as Liquor Licenses ((604) 387-1254, for suspect night clubs), Travel Services ((604) 660-3544, for shady travel agents) and Motor Dealer Licensing ((604) 387-5433, for used car salesmen). The regulators and their investigators can rarely comment on the actions of a particular person or company – that's confidential – but they can tell you the policies and laws that are supposed to be followed. Armed with that information, you can direct your research to the areas that should be examined.

Everything from banks and charities to toxic waste and bingo is regulated and has to follow a set of immutable guidelines. Determine what the guidelines are, and you're halfway there.

SEARCH WARRANTS

THANKS TO THE EFFORTS of Vancouver *Sun* crime reporter Kim Pemberton, search warrants issued in British Columbia are becoming much easier for researchers to obtain.

But once you have them: beware. The information contained in a warrant can make for exciting and intriguing stories, and can be a fine source of background information to a crime. The information can also be illegal to publish or broadcast.

When the police in a criminal investigation need information that they suspect lies behind closed doors, whether in an office or a home, they have to convince a judge or a justice of the peace that they have reasonable grounds to believe the information exists. The police have to detail those "reasonable grounds" on their application for a search warrant. Usually the information contained in the warrant is candid and explicit – the cops have to make their case, so they outline everything they know.

Search warrant applications used to be secret, but a groundbreaking judgment by the Supreme Court of Canada granted the public access in 1982. Once a search has been executed, and the police have grabbed and filed whatever evidence they believe exists, the warrants become public documents. The information requesting warrants is filed at the office of the Justice of the Peace serving the location where the warrant was served. This office is usually at the local provincial court house. (See the blue pages of your phone book for court house addresses, and see COURTS.) Researchers merely have to show up at the office and ask to see the warrant.

That's how it works on paper. But Justices of the Peace in B.C. haven't made the warrants easy to get. At the time of this writing, researchers still had to know the precise time the warrant was executed, and the location of the premises searched. Justices of the Peace were loathe to search files for busy researchers, and at times refused to release information on the grounds that the J.P. who had dealt with a particular warrant was on holidays.

Unless researchers knew that a warrant had been served – usually from information provided by a friendly police officer or lawyer – and could find the justice who had dealt with the matter, they were out of luck. Hunting for search warrants was frustrating and time-consuming. Information from warrants has provided the background material for a host of stories in B.C. – from raids on the offices of Vancouver lawyers suspected of money-laundering to investigations into the finances of the Vancouver Food Bank – but many reporters either didn't know they could get access to the warrant, or just found it too much bother to try.

The *Sun's* Pemberton spends a lot of her day hanging around Vancouver police headquarters at 222 Main Street, or across the street at the provincial court house, digging for information on her beat. Pemberton figured she wasted enough time trying to convince recalcitrant J.P.s to help her find search warrants, and, with a researcher from the CTV *National News*, she began a process that is opening the doors to search warrants throughout this province. Pemberton requested that the Chief Judge of the Provincial Court of B.C., His Honour I.B. Josephson, remind J.P.s of their duty to release search warrants – specifically documents entitled "Information to Obtain a Search Warrant (Form 1)," "Warrant to Search (Forms 5 and 5.1)," and "Report to a Justice (Form 5.2)."

The judge issued a memo to J.P.s reminding them of the law, but Pemberton still ran into problems. So she complained again.

Tony Sheridan was the assistant deputy minister in charge of the Court Services Branch for the B.C. Ministry of the Attorney General. Pemberton sent him a letter saying the judge's memo hadn't fixed things.

"In B.C.'s court system there does not appear to be any rules or uniform system in place governing storage, filing, and public access to search warrants," she wrote. "J.P.s are left to decide their own system of registering and keeping track of search warrants files. It has been our experience that J.P.s are reluctant to share this information with journalists. Most of the time our inquiries are referred to the investigating authorities. The result is the right of access to public documents is effectively denied."

She asked that a centralized filing system for search warrants be created, "on-line and accessible by the public." And, realizing that government bureaucracies would need steroids to beat slugs in a foot race, she prompted the A-G to set up a file of photocopies for search warrants, available on request in the filing area of Provincial Court registries.

A bold move, but not unique for the feisty Pemberton. She was relatively new to her beat, but her research had already taken her to the streets to investigate the murder of Vancouver prostitutes, and to back alleys to hunt for pimps preying on kids.

The Attorney General's office reacted promptly. Court administrator Joan Percival instituted a system for Vancouver Provincial Court in which all search warrants available to the public are filed in a binder kept under the front counter of the Justice of the Peace offices at 222 Main Street. Other court houses were expected to follow Percival's lead. If your local court house or Justice of the Peace doesn't cooperate with your requests, a letter to Sheridan, (Ministry of Attorney General, Parliament Buildings, Victoria, B.C. V8V 1X4) should help.

Now, a word of caution: just because you have the warrant doesn't mean you can tell people what you know. The Criminal Code of Canada was recently amended to restrict publication of search warrants.

Section 443.2(1) of the code says:

Every one who publishes in a newspaper or broadcasts any informa-tion with respect to

(a) the location of the place searched or to be searched, or

(b) the identity of any person who is or appears to occupy or be in possession or control of that place or who is suspected of being involved in any offence in relation to which the warrant was issued,

without the consent of every person referred to in paragraph (b) is, unless a charge has been laid in respect of any offence in relation to which the warrant was issued, guilty of an offence punishable on summary conviction.

The restriction doesn't completely hobble reporters, but they should take care. Pemberton used search warrant information in 1989 to determine the facts behind a story that was headlined "Lawyers' offices raided in search." The headline was in big type, and the story said that the raids had been conducted on two law offices suspected of being involved in the laundering of drug money. A juicy story, but it did not contain a hint of the identities of the lawyers involved, so the public was left to wonder about which lawyers might be implicated. Of the five Ws in a news story, the "who" and the "where" were missing, but Pemberton ensured she was safe from prosecution under the restrictions of the Criminal Code.

SOURCES

THE TITLE DOESN'T REFER to secret government Deep Throats who will meet you in underground garages if you leave a red flag in the balcony flower pots. Instead, it refers to a bi-annual publication called *Sources*, which is worth its weight in loose-lipped bureaucrats. *Sources* is produced as a for-profit enterprise by Toronto publisher Barrie Zwicker, and while it's designed to make money for its owners, it's free to working journalists. It contains almost 300 pages of public affairs contacts for governments, industries, academics, and activists of all stripes who purchase listings in hopes that researchers will contact them for information. *Sources* also carries a handy guide to contacts on Parliament Hill: cabinet ministers, MPs, and Senators.

Listings are cross-referenced by topic and in alphabetical order, so the information is easy to find. And many of the listings contain home phone numbers for contacts – an essential tool for researchers who need information outside office hours.

Sources began as a few pages in each issue of *Content*, the national news media magazine, then split off in 1977 to become an independent and essential service for anyone looking for information. (If this sounds breathless and promotional, well, it is. I've used *Sources* to get home numbers of information officers for the Canadian Security and Intelligence Service 10 minutes to deadline, and to find information from organizations and companies that I didn't know existed until I saw the listing in the magazine.)

The magazine is sold in some bookstores, and carries a $30 cover price ($50 a year for a subscription), but Zwicker will add your name to his mailing list for no charge if you write him on a piece of your news organization's letterhead proving that you are "employed full time in an editorial capacity for a newspaper, magazine, radio or television station or cable TV operation, [or are] a recognized stringer or correspondent and/or recognized freelancer." Other researchers have to pay.

Many of the sources listed are advocacy groups, and as with any information provided by such groups, you have to take it with a large dose of salt. The listing on "Abortion" offers you The Alliance For Life and the Canadian Abortion Rights Action League, among others, so you might have to contact several groups before getting all sides. Nevertheless, *Sources* will save time and money, and will help you find what you're looking for, even if you're not sure what that is. Write to:

> *Sources*
> 9 Nicholas Street
> Suite 402
> Toronto, Ont.
> M4Y 1W5

TEN-K

SOMETIMES INFORMATION on a company in B.C.'s backyard isn't immediately available at home. When that happens, you might have to look further afield to get the goods – at times you have to leave the country. That's what former Vancouver *Sun* business editor George Froehlich had to do in 1980 to ferret out the facts behind a massive megaproject that made an already wealthy expatriate U.S. businessman a lot wealthier.

Edgar Fosburgh Kaiser Jr. was born to money. The Harvard-graduate grandson of industrialist Henry Kaiser – Kaiser Steel, Kaiser Aluminum, Kaiser Cement, Kaiser Industries – moved to Canada in the 1970s to run Kaiser Resources, holder of coal-mining rights to a large chunk of B.C.'s interior. Young Kaiser had flipped the Denver Broncos football team, pocketing an estimated $40 million profit, and was dividing his time between Denver and Vancouver, with down time spent on his yachts and his Orcas Island estate. But, as Jimmy Pattison says, money is just a way of keeping score, and in early 1980 Edgar Jr. figured out a way to make more.

Bill Bennett's government had recently started an exercise in people's capitalism. Several Crown-owned companies and holdings had been privatized, controlled by a company called the B.C. Resources Investment Corporation. Every citizen of the province was granted five free shares of BCRIC, and the premier advised the public to hold on to their shares, because their value would go nowhere but up. The shares originally went on the market for $6. Since then, BCRIC has had a name change and those who heeded Bennett's advice have seen the value of their shares plummet to less than a dollar a piece.

But in 1980 BCRIC controlled hundreds of millions of dollars in capital, and was looking for stuff to buy. Anxious BCRIC-buyers learned in September of that year that the company was purchasing controlling interest in Kaiser Resources. It was a cautious, hesitant venture. The company was stable, and market analysts said the BCRIC buy was about as daring and beneficial to B.C.'s economy as putting the money into a sock. While it didn't benefit the average British Columbian, it did add sparkle to Kaiser's riches.

An information circular provided to shareholders of Kaiser Resources showed that Edgar owned almost 900,000 shares and share-options in his company. Kaiser Resources had been trading at less than $30 a share, and BCRIC was offering $55 a share to take over the corporation. On paper, Edgar stood to make a heck of a swell profit.

Now, there's nothing unusual in the head of a company owning shares in his own firm. Investors might even be suspicious of company presidents who don't trust their own company enough to invest at least some family assets. But the question was this: When did Edgar Fosburgh Kaiser Jr. buy his shares and exercise his options? Had he held them all along, or did he start buying when he learned that BCRIC was thinking of buying him out? It was known that BCRIC had, earlier that year, failed to exercise an option to buy Kaiser shares, so the questions weren't just the suppositions of cynical news reporters.

Some of the information was available from Insider Trading Reports (see VANCOUVER STOCK EXCHANGE) but Froehlich wanted as many particulars and specifics as he could find. For that, he turned to Washington, D.C. Kaiser Resources did business in the U.S., and, as a public company, it was forced under U.S. law to make a lot more information public than Canadian laws demand. Public companies doing business in the U.S., or connected to U.S. firms, must file quarterly and annual reports to the federal Securities Exchange Commission, detailing the stock transactions of key shareholders.

The annual report, known as a 10-K, revealed that Kaiser had, in fact, gone on a buying spree shortly after BCRIC's original option had fallen through. Edgar Kaiser had snapped up an extra 200,000 shares during the previous six months. That meant that Kaiser would pocket an extra $5 million by selling his inflated shares to BCRIC. He wasn't alone. The 10-K showed that a group of Kaiser executives had also purchased $11 million worth of shares and options during the previous six months. A timely buy – the value of those shares doubled with the BCRIC takeover, and the executives increased their own wealth by up to $1 million each, just by some skillful investment.

On paper, of course, using inside information on a company to make a profit is a crime. Froehlich was justifiably proud of his findings. His front-page story said: "Edgar Kaiser Jr. stands to increase his personal wealth by $5.6 million because of stock transactions in the six months preceding the announcement by the B.C. Resources Investment Corp. that it plans to take over Kaiser Resources." His story also quoted former NDP justice critic Alex Macdonald saying that, if there was a leak of information, "the BCRIC shareholders have a right to know who leaked and who benefited from the leak." But B.C. law-enforcers – the ones who also operate the Vancouver Stock Exchange – seem to have a hard time convicting anyone of substance of insider trading. An investigation was launched, but Kaiser and his executives were cleared of any wrongdoing.

Kaiser was later appointed chairman of the Bank of B.C., but didn't have as much luck as a banker. The bank that once used Lorne Greene in TV commercials promoting itself as Canada's Western bank fell on hard times, was bought out and became a subsidiary of the Bank of Hongkong. Froehlich moved to CBC's *The Journal*, then later became executive news producer at television station CKVU.

The Securities Exchange Commission is still in Washington,

D.C. It uses more than 180 forms, including the 10-K, to file information away on the companies it regulates, and I wouldn't try to outline them all here. The INVESTIGATIVE REPORTERS AND EDITORS *Reporter's Handbook* offers an excellent summary of information available from the SEC. With Free Trade the logical outcome of the worldwide merger and takeover phenomenon, anyone looking for information about Canadian business operations should keep in mind the various sources of information available from the SEC.

The 10-Q form, also known as the Quarterly Update, must be filed within 45 days after the end of each fiscal quarterly period. That means the information in the 10-Q is more current, but, unlike the 10-K, the Quarterly Update is not audited before filing, which means that generally accepted accounting practices have not necessarily been followed. 10-Qs disclose legal proceedings involving the company and changes in business operations, such as long-term contracts and new financial arrangements.

Looking for more recent information about a company which has undergone changes in ownership or finances? The 8-K form, aka Current Update, must be filed within 15 days of any important changes.

Hunting for major shareholders? The SEC's Schedule 13-D (also called the Sale of Securities form) discloses people or companies owning more than five percent of the securities of a public company that is either listed on a stock exchange or is worth more than $1 million and has 500 or more stockholders. It gives information on securities, the source of funds for the purchase, and the purchaser. If the buyer is a company, the information includes the directors and/or partners of the company involved, including subsidiary or parent firms.

And here's one which can provide hours of fun for Canadian reporters stymied in their efforts to find the earnings of Canadian executives. Proxy Statements filed with the SEC disclose salaries of directors and top officers earning more than $40,000 a year. Most large Canadian businesses are connected to U.S. parents, partners, or subsidiaries. So, while there is no access to salaries under Canadian law, the information is available just south of the border. Information from the Securities Exchange Commission is available by phone from the reference department at 1-202-272-7450. Several computer data bases offer access to SEC information. Or write the SEC at 500 N. Capitol St., Washington, D.C., USA, 20549.

UNIVERSITIES

VETERAN LABOUR REPORTER Rod Mickleburgh (the *Sun*, the *Province*, CBC TV) has a bulletin board in the kitchen of his East Vancouver home which holds scores of headlines, lovingly cut out of newspapers and magazines, all containing the word "expert."

"NDP will win, experts say." "NDP will lose, experts predict." "Experts warn of problems." "Sell now, experts say."

Mickleburgh knows that experts say a lot of things, and that the news media too often relies on alleged "experts" to tell them what's going on out there. The U.S. magazine *Mother Jones* began 1990 with an in-depth study of the experts used on U.S. network TV news and current affairs shows, which found that the news media in that country mostly relies on a tiny handful of men to give a "balanced and impartial" view to the mostly political events of the day. Trouble is, when the experts start appearing on the same shows, they lose their impartiality, and instead become minor celebrities themselves. Instead of offering balance and objectivity, they will often use their televised platform to espouse their own views, and to defend those views against people who might think otherwise.

In Vancouver in the mid 1970s and early 1980s, an organization called the Fraser Institute generated a lot of headlines, offering pronouncements on economic issues of the day. The Fraser Institute billed itself as an economic "think tank," and there was always someone around the institute to pick up the phone and offer instant expertise. Reporters assigned to get "reaction stories" to things like budgets and labour-management unrest would automatically phone the Fraser Institute and seek the comments of its experts. Invariably, the comments would reflect a "conservative" tone, but the expertise was presented in news pages as unbiased and objective because it wasn't based on an obvious political or economic bias.

We knew that the B.C. Federation of Labour wasn't "objective" – it was left of centre and, hence, pro-NDP. The Employers' Council of B.C. was the flip side – right of centre, capitalist, and pro-Socred. But the pronouncements of the Fraser Institute were unsullied by political labels. Instead, institute spokespeople were referred to as economists or, as Mickleburgh's collection shows, experts.

That is, for a time. After more than four years of reaching instantly for my phone to seek opinion from the experts of the Fraser Institute, a question that should have popped into my head much earlier finally dribbled its way into my consciousness: Who are these guys?

Institute director Michael Walker had always been friendly and helpful, even offering instant analysis when phoned at home in his bed. But when I visited him with the question, he became hesitant. "We're a think tank," he said.

But where do you get your money?

"From donations."

Donations from who?

"From corporate donors and private donors."

How much comes from corporations?

"Why are you asking me this?"

Why hasn't anyone, including me, asked you this before?

Walker paused. He looked down at the ground. "Good question," he said.

The Fraser Institute had received charitable status (see CHARITIES) from the federal government on the grounds that its purpose was "preparation, publication and distribution of treatises on economic matters of current concern. This involves the commissioning of work by academics and the authorship of its own staff economists," according to information provided to Revenue Canada. (The tax people in Ottawa will give you some information about companies and societies in a form called a Public Information Return T3010. That document lists the society's operating revenue and expenditures, including wages to society staff members.) The information provided by Revenue Canada already told me that the Fraser Institute had collected more than $800,000 to spread its word in 1982. However, the federal government would not tell me where the money came from. That information is not public.

Walker, to his credit – and to my surprise – did tell me. There were private donors all right. Hundreds of institute supporters had sent in a total of $17,000 in membership fees and donations. But the bulk of the money came from corporate supporters who read literally like a corporate Who's Who of Canadian business, chipping in almost half a million dollars in tax-deductible donations, while a group of Canadian and U.S. business foundations kicked in another quarter million.

Money had poured in from corporate head offices throughout the land, everywhere from banks and breweries to transportation companies and food giants, with more coming in from oil companies, paper factories, logging and mining interests, and real estate developers. Even the Southam and Thomson newspaper chains had added to the institute's coffers. The Fraser Institute called itself "non-profit" – hence the charitable tax status – but the corporations donating to it were giving money to further their own aims and ambitions, which were simple: making a profit. The same "non-profit" tag could be applied to the public relations departments of the corporate donors. They don't make money by themselves, but they exist as part of a corporate entity designed to make money. Now, few people argue anymore about the sin of making money, but the Fraser Institute had supported and even suggested political strategies which would maximize profits for industry while abandoning social programs. That left some people wondering if the Fraser Institute was anything more than a mouthpiece for big business. Walker said he hadn't been "bought" by anyone, but he did agree that companies donated to the institute because they believed that most of what the Fraser Institute did would increase their profits.

The short-lived Solidarity Coalition, a broad-based organization made up of labour, clerics, academics, and others opposed to the "fiscal restraint" programs of former premier Bill Bennett, conducted its own study of the institute, and concluded in a report that the supporters of the Fraser Institute "are the very large powerful corporations who overwhelmingly dominate the economy of this country."

Michael Walker and his Fraser Institute are still around, but reporters don't phone them as much as they did, and when they do, the more sophisticated newsies put the comments into perspective, dropping the "expert" label and referring to the institute as corporate-funded. But there are still lobbyists and pseudo-experts around every corner in this era of "spin doctors" and media manipulators, so it's still easy to get burned.

Instead of relying on suspiciously innocuous "charitable institutions" and "think tanks," why not go to where the academics hang out and find some real "experts"? The universities in this province employ hundreds of helpful people who have studied the issues involved, and who are usually willing to reveal their personal biases, inherent in anyone's "expertise."

The University of B.C. even produces a Faculty Experts Guide, available from its public relations department, which helps guide anxious researchers through the maze of academia. Looking for someone to talk about biotechnology? There, on page 293, is a list of half a dozen leaders in their field. The directory lists office and home telephone numbers, essential for researchers battling night-time deadlines. The guide lists experts for Shakespeare, divorce, red tide, and native Indian legal questions – 310 pages of instantly accessible experts. Yes, there are even people who will talk about economic matters, in case Michael Walker isn't answering his phone that day.

Simon Fraser University and the University of Victoria also

have leading experts in their fields – U Vic's Murray Rankin co-authored the guide to freedom of information (see **ACCESS TO INFORMATION**) and SFU's criminology department can help turn a routine cop story into a thoughtful and worthwhile story. Community colleges throughout B.C. – listed in your local telephone book – also employ hundreds of experts in their fields who are willing to speak to researchers by phone.

A note here to publishers and editors of community newspapers: having trouble filling your editorial pages? Running out of ideas for things to comment on? Take a look at your local universities and colleges. You'll find experts on topics you didn't know existed, people eager to write something to let their community in on what they know.

Every university and community college employs public relations personnel to help you find who or what you're looking for. Call them. And produce another headline for Rod Mickleburgh.

University of B.C. Public Relations:
(604) 228-3131

Simon Fraser University Public Relations:
(604) 291-3210

University of Victoria Public Relations:
(604) 721-7636

VANCOUVER
STOCK EXCHANGE

IT BEGAN AS A PARTY to promote a company catering to the whims of the rich and famous. It ended with wiretaps, police raids on brokerage houses throughout the country, and big losses for a man who dreamed of getting rich by renting dreams.

Word of the party reached the CBC television newsroom December 1, 1986, from a public relations consultant who had been hired to spread the good word. Assignment editor Duncan Speight took the call – Viva nightclub in downtown Vancouver was to be the site of a bash that evening with a champagne fountain, ice sculptures, a bevy of beautiful women, expensive cars, and munchies to die for. It was all to promote a new company called Rent-a-Dream, operated by an entrepreneur called Brett Salter. Would the CBC be interested in covering it?

Speight didn't see it as a news story, but he knew I was single and always looking for a cheap night out, so he suggested I drop by with a cameraman and take a look. It was 2 p.m. I phoned Salter's car phone to get a bit of background. It didn't sound like a news story to me either, but I decided I might as well be prepared and at least pretend to look like a reporter. Salter said he was opening a Vancouver office for a company called Rent-a-Dream which would line up expensive cars, yachts, jets, even dates with Hollywood stars for anyone who could afford a night of luxury.

"The rich and famous. That's basically who we're catering to," he said. But Salter didn't sound rich and famous himself. Instead of the self-assured, languid tone of the haughtily wealthy, he sounded like a salesman, a huckster. He refused to reveal any details about himself – "just say that Brett Salter is a very wealthy man" – and precious little about his company. Salter said he would consent to an interview that night, and told me this was a lucky break for a Vancouver reporter because he had turned down requests for interviews "dozens of times" from the TV show *Lifestyles of the Rich and Famous*.

I didn't have to be a rocket scientist to suspect that Salter sounded too weird to be true.

He gave me a telephone number for Rent-a-Dream in Vancouver, but the telephone was answered by a secretary who said "Park Resources" when she picked up the phone. The producer of *Lifestyles of the Rich and Famous* in New York checked her staff, and reported that no one had ever heard of Brett Salter or a company called Rent-a-Dream. The business pages of the Vancouver *Sun* showed that Park Resources was a publicly traded company on the Vancouver Stock Exchange, and I set out to look for something to find.

Every company doing business on the Vancouver Stock Exchange must submit copies of prospectuses, press releases, and any other information that the company has made available to prospective investors. Those files are available for viewing by the public at the fourth floor of the VSE tower at 609 Granville Street. The exchange charges $4 for each file viewed. Interested people must visit the exchange in person – information is not given over the telephone. The public relations department of the VSE (604-689-3334) will provide some information on the activities of the exchange, and a PR official said that Park Resources had been all but dormant for months, trading at an asking price of 50 cents a share. However, during the past month the price of the stock had risen to $2.20 a share – an increase of almost 350 percent.

The file on Park Resources contained press releases announcing that franchises for Rent-a-Dream had already been opened in

Toronto and Los Angeles. Phone calls to Toronto and Los Angeles found no listing for a company called Rent-a-Dream, and entertainment editors for the Toronto *Star* and Los Angeles *Times* said they'd never heard of such a company. The prospectus for Park Resources listed a personal computer. . . and nothing else. The file also contained a photocopied "catalogue" of available services, including lunch and dinner dates with recognizable Hollywood film stars. But a phone call to Actors Equity in Los Angeles gave me the stars' business agents, and the agents denied any connection to Rent-a-Dream or to Brett Salter. The agents also didn't know who Brett Salter was.

A few blocks south of the VSE tower, at 865 Hornby Street, are the offices of the B.C. Securities Commission, the government body that regulates the actions of investors and stock sellers. Publicly traded companies must divulge the identities of "insiders" to the commission's Superintendent of Brokers – affectionately known as the SOB in the trade. Insiders are said to be company directors or key employees who have inside knowledge of the activities of the company. It's against the law for those people to use their inside knowledge to make money from company shares if the public doesn't have access to the same knowledge.

At least, that's how it's supposed to work. High-profile cases like New York's Ivan Boesky have made "insider trading" a household term, and movies like Wall Street (remember Michael Douglas' character advising that "Greed is good"?) portray the securities commission as always getting their men. But getting convictions for insider trading is tough. The B.C. commission charged former premier Bill Bennett with insider trading in 1989, maintaining that he used inside knowledge of the activities of a company called Doman Industries to unload his shares in the company, avoiding a multi-million dollar loss. But Bennett wasn't a director or employee of Doman Industries. The B.C. commission claimed that Bennett must have received inside information about Doman shares, but was unable to prove the allegation, and Bennett was not convicted.

The SOB maintains files of insider traders, available to the public for a fee of $6 for each file searched. The files contain lists of directors and key employees who hold shares in the firm. But those are the only insiders listed. Major shareholders – like Bennett was in Doman – are not listed.

The insider trading report on Park Resources didn't reveal much, but the file also contained a report advising that the company had purchased Rent-a-Dream the previous month – around the same time the value of the shares began to rise – and was actively promoting the new acquisition by offering franchises in Rent-a-Dream for $100,000 apiece.

By then, offices were closing down for the day.

That night, Salter was true to his word. Viva was packed with the Vancouver glitterati and their hangers on, sucking champagne, comparing expensive watches and suntans, leaving their BMWs at the door for the valet to park. A spotlight had been rented to light up the night sky, the canapes were delicious, the women were thin. Salter arrived in a red Lamborghini, and I asked the valet if I could take a look inside the car. The automobile's registration was sitting in the glove compartment. It showed the car was registered to an Ontario company called Jazz Investments.

Inside the club, the cameraman shot footage of the Vancouver investment community mingling with itself, then we prepared to interview Salter. After the first few innocuous questions, Salter bristled at being asked if his company was little more than a dream itself. He maintained that Rent-a-Dream was a thriving business, and that it had assets other than a private computer.

Like what?

"Like my car outside," he said.

The next day, I phoned the Registrar of Companies for Ontario (see **REGISTRAR OF COMPANIES**) and learned that Jazz Investments had folded the previous year, and had not paid its Ontario tax bill. The CBC carried my report that night. Unknown to me, the RCMP were already looking at Salter, and the next day police received permission to mount a wiretap on Salter's phone. Police raided brokerage houses across Canada in 1987, claiming – according to search warrants – that "Salter and his associates had illegally and improperly traded blocks of Park Resources between themselves." The police maintained that the value of Park Resources had been driven up artificially in a scam to woo prospective investors. But Salter's promotion didn't work. Within days of the CBC report, Park Resources' shares plummeted to 48 cents. Rent-a-Dream remained just that – a dream.

VANCOUVER SUN
and PROVINCE

NEWSPAPER PEOPLE call it the daily miracle: each day, a new product with tens of thousands of words, thousands of facts, figures, and photos. A product designed to be read, or skimmed, or passed over, then thrown out with other garbage of the day. (Or, in the 90s, to be recycled as soon as pulp and paper plants can get de-inking machinery on stream.)

Reporters and editors are supposed to keep the facts about their areas of expertise in their heads, and in their own files. That's what they're paid for – knowledge, the ability to gather knowledge, and the ability to tell stories. A good reporter and researcher values not only content but context. The history of a person or the background leading to a news event help readers put things into perspective. But one reporter or editor might deal with thousands of stories a year, and it's hard to keep track of just what scalawag did what to who, and when. No human brain can keep all those facts straight.

At Vancouver's two daily newspapers, the Vancouver *Sun* and the *Province*, the newsrooms are in opposite ends of the Pacific Press building at 2250 Granville Street. Reporters and editors share the same entrances to the building, share the cafeteria and even the washrooms. But the newsrooms, the heart of the news production process, are separated by a long hallway, and journalists who work for one newspaper don't dare venture into the competition's newsroom.

If the newsrooms are the heart of the newspapers, then the library in the middle of the connecting hallway acts as the genetic memory. Pacific Press employs a dozen librarians and clerks whose job is to file stories away, to be called up when an anxious reporter, facing a pressing deadline seconds away, needs the background to a story, or the spelling of a name. Stories are cross-referenced under more than 70,000 listings and key-words (see **COMPUTER DATABASES**). If a reporter needs to know just how many fishing boats were lost at sea last year, or the name of the latest cabinet member caught in a conflict of interest, a librarian punches a few words into a computer, and the stories which have appeared in the newspapers are printed out.

In the old days, newspaper stories were photocopied and cross-referenced into paper files, with each file microfiched annually to save space. That process has now been replaced by computers, which store the information in mechanical memories. You won't find paper files any more at the *Sun* and *Province*, nor will you find bound volumes of back issues. Instead, librarians bathed in the glow of video-display terminals search the computer memory, calling up a computer print-out of yesterday's news.

It's an invaluable tool for researchers. Unfortunately, unlike most of the tools detailed so far, access to the Pacific Press library is not free to the public. Newspapers are produced to make money for the companies which own newspapers, and newspaper libraries are chiefly designed to assist in that process. Hence, staff members of the *Sun* and *Province*, as well as the news cooperative Canadian Press, have free access to the library. But at the time of this writing, the newspapers charged outside researchers $35 per visit to use the library. As with all computer databases, the Pacific Press library is cheapest to use if you have a good idea of what you're looking for already. To book an appointment at the library, call (604) 732-2605.

For researching on the cheap, there are ways around that fee. The downtown branch of the Vancouver Public Library carries microfilm copies of past issues of both newspapers. If you know the date of a story you're looking for (see ZEN), it's easy and free to visit the library and search through the microfilm. The VPL also maintains its own clipping files, a freely available source of prime research material. The sociology section of the library keeps files on everything from sports to religion, while you'll find background on B.C. politics in the North-west History division, and clippings on businesses (see WHO OWNS WHAT) are maintained in the Business and Economics division.

Microfilm copies of other B.C. daily newspapers are usually available in urban libraries (Victoria, Kamloops, Kelowna, etc.), again, free of charge. And many librarians develop their own indexes for newspapers serving their areas. I was able to track down my family background by finding an old obituary notice in a back issue of a microfilmed newspaper in Newfoundland.

Vancouver's three television news operations – CBC, BCTV and CKVU – also maintain their own private libraries to help their journalists locate old stories. Again, these are private libraries, and understaffed, and they do not perform work for the public. For anyone looking for a videotape of an old TV news story: forget it, unless you're willing to spend hundreds of dollars for each minute of videotape. The stations are besieged daily by callers hoping for a copy of a news story. The tapes are kept, but it costs big bucks to produce TV news, and the stations can't afford to tie up an editing booth to make copies of stories for the public without a hefty charge.

There are private companies in Vancouver which do record news and current events from TV and radio broadcasts. In Vancouver, Crossley Communications offers what it calls an "electronic press clipping" service, recording and selling news and current affairs programs to public relation firms. The service is run by former radio reporter Stan Crossley (at (604) 294-8252) who says he will sell tapes to the public "under certain conditions."

And, a tip to anyone who thinks they might want a videotape copy of a newscast: tape it yourself on your home VCR or audio tape-deck the day it's broadcast. As an assignment editor with the CBC who had to answer phone calls from the public, I lost count of the number of calls from unhappy parents who hoped to acquire a tape of their child who happened to be on the TV news show the previous night. They weren't able to pay the fee charged by the station, and they berated themselves for not thinking of taping the broadcast when it ran.

WHO OWNS WHAT?

WRITING AN EXPOSÉ about the company that owns your newspaper is not a good way to get ahead in business. But that's what happened when I stumbled across a name connected to the corporate owners of the Vancouver *Sun*. It was my first attempt at unraveling inter-corporate ownership and the connections of backroom big businessmen, and although the task originally appeared daunting, it wound up being laughably easy. The only trouble was, I wasted a lot of time before figuring out the easy route.

First, some background. The *Sun* had recently been purchased by a company called Southam Inc. For years the paper had been owned by a company called FP Publications, a national newspaper chain. In Vancouver, FP had a partnership with Southam. FP published the afternoon *Sun*, while Southam owned and published the morning *Province*. On paper the chains competed with each other, but they found it cheaper to share a building and printing presses.

In 1979, Thomson bought FP Publications. The following year, FP died. It was the start of a worldwide series of corporate takeovers and mergers. Newspapers were not exempt. Southam and the giant Thomson business empire chain bought, traded, and killed a number of newspapers across Canada. Once the newsprint dust had settled, newspaper reporters throughout the country were without jobs and competition in most cities was eliminated. Control of the *Sun* had passed from Thomson to Southam, which made Southam Inc. the sole owner of Vancouver's two daily papers.

But what was this entity called Southam Inc.? Frankly, the high-priced reporters in Vancouver – the men and women owned and controlled by the company (myself included) didn't know. And didn't much think about it. The papers kept on coming out daily, and nothing much had changed. My paycheque still arrived in my mailbox every two weeks, only now it was signed by a company called Southam Inc.

In 1982 the Southam name popped up again. Pay-TV had just been introduced to the country, greatly expanding the number of television stations available to cable subscribers. It was a big news story, and I was assigned to write a report on the new services which would soon come on stream. Competition to win a broadcasting license (see CRTC) had been fierce. Roy Thomson – later known as Lord Thomson of Fleet – had once described a broadcasting license as a license to print money, and big business saw pay-TV as a cash cow.

One of the bidders which had won a license was called C-Channel, an arts and entertainment television station which would pipe theatre, opera, and other "cultural" TV productions into the country's homes – for a fee. C-Channel had delivered a package of promotional material to newsrooms, hyping its services. The material noted that C-Channel was owned by a company called Lively Arts Market Builders, aka LAMB. The chairman of the board of this soft and fluffy acronym was a chap called Hamilton Southam. One of the directors was Wilson Southam.

Southam. The question popped into my mind: who are these guys? I asked around the newsroom but no one knew much except that the company signed what was cynically known as "the only byline that counts – the one on our paycheque." I suggested to city editor Vaughn Palmer that I take a look at the Southam clan and its holdings, and the story was approved.

So . . . where to begin? The only references to Southam in newspaper clippings (see VANCOUVER SUN AND PROVINCE, COM-PUTER DATABASES) spoke of it as a newspaper chain. I knew that already. The Vancouver Public Library had an ANNUAL REPORT for Southam Inc., which noted that the company had made profits from a number of its trade magazines and from its 33 percent share of the Canadian edition of *TV Guide* magazine. Money had also flowed in from its 30 percent share in something called Selkirk Communications. Interesting... but what was Selkirk Communications?

The very helpful librarians showed me a copy of a book called *The Blue Book of Canadian Business*. The *Blue Book* provides capsule profiles of scores of Canadian companies, their owners and directors. Similar information was also available from "Financial Post Cards" – a service of the *Financial Post* newspaper. Again, capsule profiles of major Canadian companies, subsidiaries, profits and loss. Information on companies connected to foreign firms is also provided in publications called *Who Owns Whom* and *Standard and Poor's Register of Corporations, Directors and Executives* – a three-volume set listing about 36,000 Canadian and U.S. companies, including biographies on major business figures.

I filled up a notebook and got confused. The picture developing was this:

Southam owned 30 percent of the voting stock – and 38 percent of the non-voting shares – in Selkirk Communications.

In turn, Selkirk owned and controlled Vancouver radio stations CKWX and CJAZ (which later became oldies station CISL). In the field, reporters from the *Sun* and *Province* competed with each other, and competed against reporters from private radio. But here, in these compendiums of Canadian big business, was proof that the profits we generated were going to the same people.

The lines of competition got even murkier. Selkirk also owned and controlled a small block of voting stock in a company called British Columbia Television Broadcasting Ltd., the company that controlled television station BCTV, and CHEK in Victoria. The block was small but, after a lot of digging, I found that Selkirk also held a fully owned subsidiary company called Castleton Investments, which also owned shares in BCTV. In all, Selkirk controlled 37 percent of the shares of BCTV. The bulk of the rest of the shares were controlled by a company called Western Broadcasting – the firm that operated the city's largest AM and FM radio stations: CKNW and CFMI. That company also owned the Vancouver Canucks hockey team.

The connections meant that the largest newsrooms in Vancouver – the *Sun*, the *Province*, BCTV, CKNW – were corporate partners. It didn't stop there. A fascinating book called the *Directory of Directors* lists the directorships held by prominent businesspeople. And it showed that the directors of the companies involved sat on the corporate boards of other media giants as well.

The process of mapping out the inter-corporate connections was tedious, confusing, and tiresome. I went looking for help, and contacted the communications department at Simon Fraser University (see UNIVERSITIES) to see if anyone there had looked into the connections. As it turned out, SFU instructor Peter Anderson, a member of the university's telecommunications research group, had spent three years wading through the maze of interlocking ownership of the Canadian communications industry. To Anderson, the corporate connections were "mind-boggling." He had produced a chart – "it's a hobby" – detailing the various connections of the country's major newspaper, television, and radio companies. The owners sat in each other's pockets, and what passed for competition to the public was actually a tightly controlled club of media giants: Southam, Thomson, Torstar (publishers of the Toronto *Star* newspaper and Harlequin romance novels, among other things), Maclean-Hunter Ltd., CHUM Ltd., and Moffat Communications.

The route I had taken to get this far, and to get a handle on the connections, took weeks of part-time digging and rooting about in files. Finally I stumbled across a publication produced by Statistics Canada called *Inter-Corporate Ownership*. The gnomes at StatsCan had crunched the information available and produced their own directory of ownership, cross-ownership, and corporate connections. StatsCan scoured all the public information available to the federal government, plus media reports and information available from foreign sources.

The directory is hefty but easy to read, and there, in simple language, was a detailed account of just what Southam owned and to whom it was connected. If I had started with StatsCan, my "investigation" would have been cut to a few days. I wish I had. *Inter-Corporate Ownership* is available at most libraries. The directory is updated every few years, so its information quickly becomes out of date (in 1989 a flurry of sales completely changed the connections of Southam, Selkirk and Western) but it's a great place to start. As well, StatsCan will often provide updates by phone. In Vancouver, phone Statistics Canada at (604) 666-3691. For areas outside Vancouver, call StatsCan toll free at 1-800-663-1551.

The story finally got written, but it took months until it was published. The men running the *Sun's* cityside didn't much want to anger their bosses – and harm their own career ambitions – by exposing backroom business dealings, but after several months, acting business editor Michael Sasges took on the story for his pages, giving it big play. Sasges never was appointed business editor.

ZEN, AND THE ART OF PUTTING IT ALL TOGETHER

AS PATRICK RIORDAN NOTED in the chapter on IRE, there is no replacement for shoeleather. And documents are no substitute for people. People make stories, and stories are about people. People also know things that might not be found in public documents. Members of trade unions will know about illegal work practices that aren't mentioned in annual reports. Neighbours know stories about people they've lived beside. Librarians will guide you through the volumes of unrelated stuff you'll have to rummage through to get the goods.

Finding the information you're looking for is just the start. Then you've got to find the people affected by that information. That means thinking about people, and not stopping until you've found the people and the human story behind the facts and statistics. I hope this book will help you get started.

Again, for researchers setting up personal libraries in this province, I'd suggest they keep these volumes on their desk:
- Overbury's *Finding Canadian Facts Fast*
- B.C. Government Phone Book
- IRE *Reporter's Handbook*
- The White Pages of your phone book
- *Sources*

They're also available at your public library, along with the other publications mentioned in this book. All you have to do is think of looking for something to find, and somewhere, someplace, is the information you seek. And please reread **DUMPSTER DIVING** for suggestions on how to keep your files in order.

Happy hunting.

Printed in Canada